Lock Down Publications and Ca$h
Presents

GETTIN' MONEY BY THE TRUCKLOAD

SUPPLY AND DEMAND

Written By
CHRISTOPHER "DIESEL" HORNEZES

First Edition 2025

Printed in the United States of America

Lock Down Publications
P.O. Box 944
Stockbridge, GA 30281
www.lockdownpublications.com

Like our page on Facebook: Lock Down Publications
www.facebook.com/lockdownpublications.ldp

Stay Connected with Us!

Text **LOCKDOWN** to 22828 to stay up-to-date with new releases, sneak peaks, contests and more…

Like our page on Facebook:
Lock Down Publications

Join Lock Down Publications/The New Era Reading Group

Visit our website:
www.lockdownpublications.com

Follow us on Instagram:
Lock Down Publications

Email Us: We want to hear from you!

Chapter 1

Early Summer, 2017

Lighting strikes lit the dark sky up like a bunch of paparazzi cameras taking pictures every five seconds or so. Thunder boomed so hard that the ground quaked. The storm wreaked havoc on the city of Chicago. It was of biblical proportions. It was as if God was angry and unleashing his fury on Chiraq.

Standing at the ledge of an opened loading dock door to a big building at the rear of a scrap-metal yard, out in the Little Village neighborhood, Pancho looked out into the torrential downpour of rain, flooding the dirt/gravel lot in front of the building. He was the owner, and he was pissed.

Pancho had been buying Grade A cocaine from a prominent Dominican family for the last five months. It was supreme, the best product in the country, and he'd gotten filthy rich off of it. Recently, he's dropped five hundred thousand for a re-up, stepping his game all the way up. It was late, and he was so livid that he was as red as a tomato. At first, he'd been hesitant with the Valdez family. They were a well-known cocaine importing/trafficking family, with the reputation of true gangsters.

His people had warned him about getting into bed with them, but Pancho wanted to get money, and in his game, if you wanted to be the best, you had to have the best. Since Pancho had made the switch from one mediocre Mexican cartel to the Valdez family, he had quadrupled his worth, then it quadrupled again. He'd been excited about establishing a connection with the boss of the big Dominican family, and had been able to secure himself a connect so that he could make Chicago have cold summers. It was his fifth re-up, and it was late.

He was born in Ecuador, but raised in Chicago, out south in the *Back of the Yards.* He came up on the streets, gangbanging, selling drugs, shooting at the opps. He's developed a reputation for being a warrior. As he did so, he had been recruiting loyal soldiers from around the city's most dangerous areas, then when his crew grew to nearly eighty men strong, he called his self-made mob *Los Hombres Hechos-The Made Men.* He even brought over other Ecuadorians from Ecuador. Pancho had visions of taking over Chicago, and all the towns and cities that surrounded the Windy City.

Dressed in a silk Versace button-up shirt, slacks, and loafers on his feet with a Cartier on his wrist, the forty-year-old looked like he was trying to be one of the characters from the eighties hit TV show, *Miami Vice*.

Standing at his side were his two main guys, Malo and Juice. They were both giants compared to their chunky five-foot-seven-inch-tall boss. Malo was athletic with long braids rocking a red and black Jordan sweat suit, with the matching Nikes on his feet. He had flawless diamond studs in his ears, flicking like the diamond chain around his neck, and the diamond-encrusted Rolex on his wrist.

Juice was lighter in weight. He was rocking a Balenciaga fit with special-edition Balenciaga Arenas on his feet. Like Malo, he was dripping in diamond jewelry.

Behind them congregated in groups, speaking mostly in Spanish amongst themselves, were forty men, all armed with pistols and choppers, waiting to get Pancho's big load of cocaine unloaded, whenever it arrived.

***

"On *erythang* I love, Joe, these niggas got me fucked up, fam!" Pancho sneered as he watched the heavy rain. "How the fuck do they feel it's cool to let a muthafucka pay half a mil' then be late with the merch?"

"They think we sweet, fam," Malo said, instigating the situation further, since he didn't like the Valdez family anyway. "I told you, we shoulda' never started fuckin' with them Dominican niggas in the first place. They ain't right, Joe."

"Straight up," said Juice, agreeing with his homeboy. "It's like you dun' forgot how they did the Rojas-Gomez cartel, Pancho. They killed Victor and his pops and his grandma! Yo' guy in Milwaukee put us on with them new thangz we got in the basement, we should've made him our coke connect, too, bro."

"I did consider that, but he ain't got that payow that the Valdez family got," Pancho told the young one. "When it comes to the business of supply and demand, when the demand is strong, the supply must be stronger. I need a strong supply so I can stay in demand, y'all feel me?"

They both nodded but gave no reply.

"It ain't about likin' who you deal with, although it's a plus when the business is conducted in the right way. As long as the money is right, man, fuck everything else. But when a half a million dollars' worth of cocaine is four hours late, then it becomes a problem," Pancho said.

"I can't een lie," Juice spoke again. "I'm happy with the new demo he put us on, there is only one thing rich muthafuckas like more than money and drugs."

Pancho and Malo both nodded their heads in agreement. They were new to the highly lucrative endeavor that Pancho had gotten his guy in Milwaukee to put them on with. It had already been making his pockets even fatter, due to the rich clientele he had that loved getting high, then busting a nut.

"Never thought we'd be doing shit like this, but it if it makes money, I'm for it," Malo said, not caring at all about what harm he and the other two were causing.

"Aye, Pancho, man, call that bitch ass nigga and ask him why the fuck we still standin' around lookin' stupid? This waitin' shit for the birds," Juice said angrily.

Pancho pulled his iPhone out and made the call to the number he had for the connect. It was answered in four rings.

"May I help you?" a man answered calmly.

Pancho snapped back, "Aye, Joe! Where the fuck is my merch at, fam? You got a nigga just sittin' here lookin' dumb 'n shit!"

"First off, *mamabicho*," the man said, disrespecting Pancho by calling him a dick-sucker. "Watch who the fuck you talking to. You really do not want no 'shomoke with me, home boy! *Secondly*, it is raining cats and dogs. I know for a fact that you looking outside right now. Bet you can't even see the fence that lines your property."

Grinding his teeth, Pancho looked towards the perimeter of his property and indeed, he could not see the chain-link fence that ran along Kedzie. All he could see were the vehicles that belonged to his guys parked right outside the loading/unloading area.

The man continued. "Don't trip, cutty. You most definitely gon' get what you got comin'. Now get the fuck up off my line."

The call ended, leaving Pancho so pissed that he turned red as a tomato. His guys looked at him and could see the vein threatening to pop out of his forehead.

"What that nigga say, Pancho?" Malo asked.

Pancho shook his head as he put his phone back into his pocket. "If I ever meet dude in person I'ma pop his ass myself, Joe."

***

Another half an hour passed before Pancho heard the sound of a truck's loud jake-brake. Looking towards the entrance to his yard, he saw headlights, seconds before he saw an eighteen-wheeler making a wide turn in. Relieved, Pancho told his guys to get ready, then patted his waistline, feeling the butt of his 9mm Beretta was tucked. He had plans to introduce the driver to the barrel of hydrofluoric acid and bury it somewhere for the Valdez family to never be able to find.

Pancho, Juice, and Malo watched the truck as it crept slowly along the muddy water-logged and bumpy path towards the building. As it reached the parking lot where Pancho's big two-tone Bentley Brooklands sat amongst the vehicles of his men, the bright light from all the tall light poles gave the three a better look at it.

Juice and Malo caught chills just looking at the old Peterbilt. Remembering the movie *Joy Ride*, starring the gone-but-not-forgotten actor Paul Walker, Pancho swore that the truck looked just like the one that the psychotic trucker in the movie drove, while trying to run down *Lewis* and his brother *Fuller.* Pancho felt a little chill go up his spine as the engine roared angrily out of the old rig's tall and loud straight stacks. Juice and Malo both imagined that they would be seeing a big, dirty heavy-set white guy with a messy beard, wearing a flannel shirt, with ripped-off sleeves, tattered jeans, cowboy boots, and a mesh truck hat hop out.

They watched as the old truck made a right swing turn, getting the forty-eight-foot-long container-style trailer lined up with the loading dock they were standing at. The brake lights came on as the truck came to a stop. They heard a loud whoosh of air come from it. It didn't move after that.

A few seconds later, they saw a figure in all black with a hoodie head, run around to the rear of the trailer, unlock the swing doors, open them both all the way up and then disappear back around the driver's side. After another loud hiss of air came again, the rig started backing up. It kept on coming until it got to the dock's doorway, lightly bumping into the rubber bum-stop at the edge.

Pancho and his men saw the wall of boxes with different tool manufacturing and industrial cleaning chemical names lined the container's rear. Pancho nearly started salivating as he thought about all the cocaine that he was about to flood Chicago with.

Yeah! Time to get rich! Let's get it! he thought.

Juice and Malo both rubbed their hands together with greedy smiles growing on their faces.

Just then, the side door to the parking lot in between the opened loading dock door and a closed one opened up just then, and in stepped an individual that was not what Pancho nor his guys had in mind. It was not a big dirty heavy-set white guy with a greasy beard wearing a flannel shirt that had ripped-off sleeves, tattered jeans, cowboy boots, and a mesh trucker hat. Who they saw stood about five-nine inches tall. Along with the baggy hooded sweat suit and black Air Forces, a black bandana tied around the bottom half of their face concealed their identity.

Pancho grew even more pissed now that the cause of his coke delivery being so late was because of a hoodlum truck driver.

"Aye, my nigga!" he shouted to the driver, with his hand on his waistline. "Fuck is you so late wit' my shit for, Joe?"

Juice and Malo were both ready to draw their guns as well. The other men stood silent, watching, wondering if bullets were about to fly.

The driver then removed the hoodie and slid the bandana down. The three gasped in shock when they saw it wasn't a man at all…but a woman…a seriously stunning woman.

Gooooooddamn! Pancho thought, with wide eyes.

Daaaaaayuuuuum, Joe! thought Juice.

Eeeeee, lil' mama bad than a muthafucka! Malo thought, licking his lips and visualizing her naked.

Seeing the stupefied looks on their face, the girl chuckled. "Lemme guess…y'all was expectin' a big fat hairy white dude in a mesh trucker hat, a plaid shirt, dirty-ass jeans, and cowboy boots, right?" she asked, sounding like a tough, yet very feminine chick.

Pancho noticed she sounded like she was from New York.

"Um…kind of," Juice admitted, smiling at the beautiful Latina.

"My bad, shorty. I ain't mean no disrespect," Pancho said.

"Naw, it's all good, yo. Can't go too fast in the rain, yah mean? My brakes won't work right. A truck crashin' into something with a trailer full of cocaine would not be good."

"I get it," Pancho said, then all went silent as the men stared at her.

"Sooooo…I do have ya' order, however, I get paid to drive, not unload."

Pancho turned to his crew and barked, "Y'all heard the pretty lady! ¡Todos a trabajar!"

Obeying their boss's word, the men formed a human conveyor system at the trailer. The first guy grabbed a box and passed in on, continuing to grab and pass in a hand-bomb unloading style. Box after box was sent then down the line towards the center of the floor.

Malo and Juice stood a few feet away from Pancho. They both watched the men work.

Pancho turned and looked at the trucker girl. He gazed at her, lusting over the beautiful woman. He wondered where she was from. She had smooth caramel-toned skin, with an amazingly gorgeous face. He could even see what looked like a light sprinkle of freckles on her cheeks. He couldn't stop himself from gawking at her.

He looked at her sexy lips and imagined how they might feel wrapped around his dick. He was sure that if he flaunted some cash that he could pull her and make her his bitch. Surely, she couldn't be making that much money driving a truck even if she was a drug trafficker.

This bitch is so bad, Joe! *I should make her mine*, Pancho thought, lusting so hard after her.

"Is there a reason you're staring at me?" she asked suddenly, startling Pancho, since she hadn't even acknowledged him, not one time.

A shit-eating grin grew on his face. "My bad, shorty. I'm just surprised by how beautiful you are. What's yo' name?"

Turning her head, the woman looked at him with her beautiful brown eyes. She started smirking at Pancho.

"In three seconds, it won't matter what my name is, *mamabicho*," she told him. Hearing her call him a cocksucker, just like the man on the phone had, made Pancho's anger flare back up.

"Bitch!" he snapped, whipping his gun out and cocking it. "Who the fuck you think you talking to like that? I'll knock yo' muthafuckin' wig off!"

Malo and Juice upped their guns and cocked them. The men hand-bombing the boxes stopped and stared. The woman started chuckling, then she started laughing, hysterically. Pancho's eyes went red.

Bitch! You think it's a game?" he snapped, wrapping his finger around the trigger. "Guess what? I win, bitch!" he then proclaimed.

But before he could pull the trigger…

BRRRRRRRRRRRRRRRRRRRRRRRRRRRRRRRRRRRRRRRRRRRRRRRRRRRRRRRRRRRRRRRRRRRRRRRRRRRRRRRRRRRRRRRRRRRRRRRRRRR!

From inside the trailer, the deafening blast of what sounded like machine guns erupted. Bullets flew through the boxes like a swarm of armored Africanized killer bees. The men that were closest to the trailer's rear were blown to pieces from hailstorms of slugs obliterating them.

Those that had managed to duck away raised their guns, aimed at the trailer, and got ready to blast whoever was inside of it, when suddenly, the glass windows in the ceiling exploded.

Thick ropes dropped down, and like the feds doing a raid, four more shooters in all black and masked up rappelled down from the roof gripping and pointing submachine guns down at them. Pancho's men that still remained alive froze in fear as the mob of shooters dropped down to the ground with their fully automatic H&K G36s, all of them with 100-round drums.

"Everybody down!" a massively tall man with broad shoulders yelled out.

"Down! Get cha'll's bitch asses down!" a big burly man that had long dreads hanging out from his mask yelled.

The door where the trucker chick came in opened up, and three more shooters in all black and masks ran in, with AR-15s fitted with monkey-nut drums.

Thinking that they were the cops, Pancho's men obeyed, dropping their guns, scared shitless as to what the hell was really going on.

Pancho, Malo, and Juice remained silent as they realized how bad a situation they were in. They had no clue what to do.

"By now, you should know you ain't getting no yaya," he heard the trucker girl say. "Drop y'all's guns, or fat-ass here is gon' lose his mind."

They obeyed, dropping their pistols and raised their hands up.

"Wh-what the fuck is this, Joe?" Pancho asked her.

"You will find out very soon, mamabicho," the trucker girl told him.

From inside the trailer, two women walked out, each holding a M134 minigun with both of their hands, with 250-round belts of 7.62mm NATO rounds that spit so many in mere seconds wrapped around their shoulders.

The four men that dropped in from the roof, and the two others all removed their masks.

"Who the fuck is y'all niggas, Joe?" Y'all think y'all can rob us and walk up outta here alive?" Malo snapped, glaring at the six big dudes, and the three females, plus the trucker chick.

BRRRRRR!

The shortest chick, high-yellow with rust-colored hair pointed her AR at him and squeezed the trigger. His entire upper body was reduced to chunks of meat.

“Anybody else care to open their mouths and get cha’ shit pushed back?” she asked, looking at Pancho and Juice.

Terrified, Juice threw all caution to the limit and made a break for it. He ran as fast as he could go towards one of the emergency exits.

Pancho watched him flee. He cursed under his breath, having contemplated making a run for it as well.

“It might look like he’s gonna get away,” said the trucker girl, still holding a fully automatic Glock 18 to Pancho’s head, “but he is not.”

Pancho’s eyes stayed on his guy. He saw that he had reached the emergency side exit and forcefully pushed the doors open. He was about to run out, when Pancho heard him scream in panic.

“!Maliante! Agarra ‘se cabrón!’,” the trucker girl yelled out suddenly.

Pancho’s eyes went wide in horror when he saw a massive Rottweiler pounce on Juice and take him to the ground.

“Aaaaggggghhhhhhhhh!” screamed Juice as the dog’s teeth sank into his shoulder, crunching and ripping his flesh. Juice screamed as the one-hundred-six-pound German killer mauled him. Pancho was powerless to help his guy. With so many guns pointed at him, all he could do was watch Juice fight a losing battle.

“Heeelp! Heeelp meee! Panchoooooo! Pleeeeease!” Juice begged as he literally felt his flesh being ripped from him.

The dog then got ahold of Juice’s throat. He bit down as hard as he could as Juice’s screams became gags. The dog’s powerful jaws put the squeeze on his windpipe. His air got cut off. His eyes started bulging, ready to pop out of their sockets, He thought his head was about to explode from pressure, when the dog suddenly snatched his head to the left. Seconds before he died, Juice felt his Adam's apple get ripped out of his throat.

Backing away from the dead man, the dog chomped and chewed, then swallowed the Adam's apple like it was a tasty treat.

Pancho was gobsmacked when he saw the Rottweiler rip his guy's throat out and eat it. Never before in real life had he ever seen anything like that.

The trucker girl chuckled as her Rottweiler trotted back towards her. Pancho used the slight distraction and punched the trucker girl in her jaw, then he took off running, terrified that at any second, he'd feel bullets hit him in the back.

As he ran, he heard the trucker chick shout to the others to hold their fire. He was relieved beyond reason, happy enough that it seemed like his legs started running faster to get him to the exit.

Out of breath already, Pancho made it to the door and threw his body at it. The door flew open, but freedom was not on the other side. Standing on the other side was a demonic-looking tiger-brindle Red Nose Pitbull. With clipped ears standing straight up, piercing green eyes locked right into him, teeth gnashing, Pancho pissed his pants in fear.

The young Pitbull started growling viciously at him. The hairs on her back stood up. She was ready to get him but obediently waited for her human to give her the word.

Pancho swallowed hard as he looked the demon dog in her eyes.

"Ahem. Yo, my man?" he heard then.

He looked up and saw the two tall and muscular men that stood right behind her, both of them with shotguns in their hands.

The men were huge! The taller one of the two stood six-six, and was built like a NBA center that spent too much time in a weightlifting gym. He had a golden-brown skin tone, long dreadlocks that hung down past his barrel chest, and a razor-sharp beard and goatee. He rocked all-black, with black biker gloves on.

The shorter one stood six-three and looked like a slightly shorter version of the dread head. He was built like a heavyweight boxer, with long braids hanging down his wide chest. On his head, he rocked a Pittsburgh fitted and had on all black. He too had black biker gloves on.

A diabolical smirk grew on his face as he saw the fear in Pancho's eye. The cold look in his bluish-gray eyes scared Pancho so much that he swore he was looking at pure evil in flesh.

"By now, you should be realizing that there is no escape," the guy with the colored eyes said, with an accent closely similar to the trucker girl's, and the woman that was on the phone. "But just in case you haven't…"

The dread head suddenly cocked back and socked Pancho in his jaw hard, knocking him clean out.

Chapter 2

Macho

Slap!

"Wakey-wakey, eggs and bakery, bitch-nigga!" said Macho after he bitch-slapped Pancho hard in the face. "I like my vic's woke and scared shitless!"

Pancho jumped awake. Immediately, he saw the two men again, standing in front of him. Behind them were five men and four women, all holding guys that were still alive, at gunpoint. The Rottweiler and the Pitbull sat obediently at the trucker girl's side, their eyes on Pancho, barely blinking. To the side of where the mob stood, he saw the trucker chick, with a slightly swollen jaw. She was staring daggers into him.

Pancho swallowed hard, then discovered that he was tied to a metal chair, stripped down to just his boxers.

"Aye? Bitch?" Macho snapped his fingers in front of Pancho's face, getting his attention. "So not only are you a creep, but you felt it was okay to punch my lady?"

Macho cocked back and rocked Pancho as hard as he could. Pancho's jaw immediately broke and sagged to the side. He screamed, then screamed even louder when he discovered how much it hurt to scream.

His woman walked up and socked him again, so hard that he farted.

"Shut the fuck up, creep ass bitch!" she yelled, then her home girl ran up on him and rocked his jaw herself.

Macho, his brother, their five childhood homies, made up the Steel City Mafia, straight out of Pittsburgh, PA's gutter. They laughed at the crazy Nuyorican.

"Check it out, Pancho. Allow me to introduce myself, I am the boogie man," Macho joked, then he nodded his head at the giant dread head standing next to him. "This is my brother, the big boogie man, whom everyone just calls Tool. The lovely lady that just socked yo' clown ass is the queen that rules my kingdom, they call her the Bad Rican," he said of the trucker girl, who now stood next to her man, glaring at Pancho. "The other Boricua one that blew so many of yo' bitch ass homies down with that minigun," he said, making Pancho look at the beautiful deep brown skinned chick, with angry slanted Asian-like eyes. "That's her homegirl, G-Baby, a.k.a. The Gangsta Boo." he then introduced the mob of goons that he and his brother had grown up with in the 4-1-2.

The side door to the building opened up just then. Macho turned his head and saw the woman who was the reason that they were there, walk in with a look on her face that said she was on a mission, as did the 12-gauge tactical Mossberg pump in her hands.

"And that beautiful black sister right there, that is the Afro-Brit. She's from Nigeria, but she grew up in England. She migrated to the states on her own, leaving her family behind after she discharged from years in the British military. She just wanted to build a life here and help her family get to the states one day. She's badass, and she is very angry with you. You have something that belongs to her, and if she doesn't get it back…ooooowee…yo' ass is grass, bitch ass nigga. You will suffer the most painful death a human being could experience. It'd be in your best interest to tell her the truth the first time, or someone here is gonna make you scream so loud that Mariah Carey might sue you for tryin' to imitate her."

The SCM and the ladies laughed at Macho.

Macho got serious then, looking Pancho in his eyes. "Now. Where are they, Pancho?"

"Wh-Where are who?" Pancho managed to ask through the agonizing pain.

The Bad Rican busted out laughing just then. "Ha! Yeeaah, nigga! I told ya' muthafuckin' ass that he would play stupid!" she hollered, teasing her man. She stood up on her tippy toes and looked up into his eyes that had always made her pussy so wet. "You owe me dinner!"

Macho shook his head. He turned his head and looked at Pancho. "You just made me lose a bet. I bet my woman that there is no way in hell after seeing what you just saw, that you would play stupid."

CRACK!

Macho cocked back and socked Pancho in the right eye so hard that it swelled shut and started turning blue almost instantly.

"I hate losing bets, especially because pieces of shit like you can't just man the fuck up and tell the truth."

Pancho whimpered. "P-Please, man! I-I got money here! You can have it all! Just let me go!"

CLICK CLACK!

The Afro-Brit stepped up and put the barrel of her gauge in his face. "Listen to me, yoo' punk bitch muthafucka!" she said, with a thick British accent. "Nobody gives a bloody toss about yoo', oor' yoo'r crying! If yoo' doo'n't tell me what the fuck I want to know, I will blow yoo'r fucking balls off!"

For emphasis, she dropped the barrel down and rammed it in his crotch.

"Oooweee," said Macho, cringing at the thought. "Yo, you better tell her what she wants to know, bruh. That shit gon' hurt!"

Pancho started crying. He'd never been so scared in his life.

G-Baby raised the mini-gun up and pointed it right at Pancho.

"Nobody wants to hear that shit, bitch-ass nigga! Shut it the fuck up, goddammit!" she demanded, with her finger around the trigger.

Pancho then peeped the Bad Rican tuck her gun into her holster on the right side of her sweats, then pulled a sharp Rambo hunting knife from the leather sheath on the other side of her sweats.

Seething with anger, she stepped forward and snapped. "Motherfucker! ¿Dónde están ellos?" she demanded to know. "I swear to fucking God, I will cut every one of your fingers off and make you eat them, pussy!"

Macho busted out laughing. "She will do it, too, yo. Believe me. I've seen her do it before."

The Afro-Brit's hand began shaking as she kept the shotty in Pancho's crotch. She wanted so badly to pop his nuts off, but if she did, all the hard work they put in to get them to that point would be for nothing.

Pancho's bladder released even more from the look the Afro-Brit's angry eyes. He was so terrified that he started crying.

The Bad Rican cocked back and rocked his jaw. "Shut the fuck up and talk, bitch!"

Macho and his posse busted out laughing at her.

"Bae, how you gon' tell the nigga to shut the fuck up and talk?"

"Ioun' fuckin' know but fuck this sick ass bastard!" she replied back, grilling Pancho with fiery eyes.

The Afro-Brit started counting down from three, wrapping her fingers around the trigger. A foul odor began permeating the air just then.

"Eeew! He shit on himself," the G-Baby said, with her lip curled up in disgust. "Shoot his nasty ass, Joe!"

Pancho then screamed, "Wait! Hold up! They're in my basement! They're in my basement!"

"Alrighty, then." Macho patted him on his shoulder. "Let's go and get them, shall we?"

***

Macho's woman cut the restraints off Pancho, then forcing him to lead the way, Macho held his AA-12 to the back of Pancho's head. Macho's woman, the dogs, G-Baby, Tool, Perry, his rusty-haired girlfriend Felicia, and the Afro-Brit all followed. City Cee, Dee, and Lacey, stood guard over Pancho's terrified men, guns trained on them, wishing any of them would try something slick.

A couple minutes later, they got to where Pancho's office was. A retina scanner was built into the wall at the side of it. As they stood in front of it, Macho, and the girls knew that what they came for was inside. An eye-retina scanner built onto the exterior of an office room screamed out that something top-secret was inside.

Pancho put his eye to the scanner. It unlocked, then he pushed the door open. Motion sensor lights came on automatically, illuminating the spacious tool room. Macho put the barrel of his cannon back to Pancho's dome, making him stay where he was. He commanded the dogs to search the room.

Dreams and Maliante obediently ran inside and did a search as they were trained to do. Macho watched them sniff around. They felt no threat was inside, but as they picked up the scent by a wall with a tool shelf in front of it, they turned back towards their owners, sat and barked once.

"Buen trabajo, mis amores!" Yessy praised, calling them back out of the room.

Macho pushed Pancho inside then.

"Open it up," Macho demanded, knowing for sure that there was a hidden space behind the wall.

Pancho hurried to the tool shelf and reached through, pressing on a false brick. The sound of air hissing came. He took a step back as the wall began to slide to the right. A steel door that was hidden behind it was revealed. Pancho opened the door up, then pointed down the stairs.

The dogs were again commanded to go check it out. They both took off down the stairs to do as told. Seconds later, Macho and the ladies all heard the terrified screams of women come from down the steps.

The Afro-Brit, the Bad Rican, G-Baby and Felicia took off for the stairs, while Macho, Tool and Perry stayed back holding Pancho, keeping their guns on him.

Pancho looked at Macho and started begging. "Please, bro. Lemme' live and I swear I'll disappear! Nobody will ever hear from me again!"

"Shut up, bitch," Tool snapped, then hit Pancho in his shit so hard that he pooped his pants even more.

Yessinia

Chloe gasped in shock when she saw nearly twenty young, terrified girls, dressed like prostitutes. They all had ankle shackles on, preventing them from going more than five feet away from where they were. From their looks, not one of them was eighteen years old.

Seeing such young women, beaten, bruised, swollen, being held as prisoners and beyond freaked out, had Yessy, her best friend G-Baby, and Felicia all heated beyond belief.

Chloe's eyes watered when she spotted the one girl she had pleaded for her bosses to help her find.

Seeing her young cousin there, she spoke in Swahili. "Taranda! Binamu! Ni mimi! Chloe," she cried, calling her cousin's name out first, then saying, "Cousin! It's me!"

Yessy and her girls saw the young Nigerian girl's eyes light up.

"Chloe!" Taranda shouted, jumping up and running to her big cousin. She ran into Chloe's arms as her eyes filled with tears of joy. "Tulikuwa kwenye sherehe ya chuo kikuu na vijana hawa walikuja na kujitolea kuvuta bangi na kunywa pamoja nasi! Tulikwenda nao na baadhi ya wanaume waliokuwa wamajificha kwenye gari wakatu chuka!" She wept as her cousin's own tears fell down her face. "Walituleta hapa na kulazimisha kuwa watumwa wa ngono!" she added.

It broke Chloe's heart to hear her cousin tell her how she and her friends were at a college party, and some random guys offered to smoke and drink with them. Foolishly, they agreed to go with the guys, only to get snatched up by more men that were hiding in a car outside of where the party was jumping off. The worst part was Taranda told Chloe that the men had forced them to become sex slaves.

The very thought of it had Chloe's heart crying. Her baby cousin had come to the United States from Nigeria on a student visa, to study medicine at one of Wisconsin's most popular colleges. She'd been helping to pay Taranda's tuition. Both of their parents had been killed by gun fire from rebels over in Kenya and they only had each other. Chloe was Taranda's only living relative in the U.S. Chloe made sure that she stayed in contact with her cousin, with daily calls and video calling.

Four weeks had passed, and Chloe hadn't heard from her cousin. She'd been texting, calling, and leaving voicemails. She was worried sick about Taranda. It was like she had seemingly disappeared.

After three more days of nothing, Chloe went to Yessy and Macho, terrified about her cousin. Yessy immediately hopped into action and used her connections in military intelligence units to help out. She knew people that could track people down and even tap into using satellites.

Macho knew a lot of people in Madison, where the girls attended college. He rode up there and started spreading around money to get any information. When he found that there were reports of young foreign girls disappearing from a wild party, he told Yessy.

Yessy fed the information to her intelligence connections. The satellite technology was put to work, and from above, the night of the party, Taranda and her friend could be seen being led out of the house towards a parking lot, where a group of men jumped out of a van, snatched them up, and sped off with them inside. The satellite was able to see exactly where they went.

From that point on, Macho called the matriarch of his family, and his brother, to help get Chloe's cousin back, and the other young ladies that had been taken.

When Macho told the head of his family Pancho's name, she immediately told him that Pancho was one of their customers. Things got even easier from there. G-Baby, who was always with Macho and Yessy, was ready to ride. Chloe, dying to get her cousin back safely, was strapped up and ready.

Pancho's re-up call came just in time. When he paid the half-million to up his order, he had no clue that he was paying for his own death.

***

Chloe spoke again. "Ni sawa Niko hapa sasa," she said, telling her little cousin that it was okay, and that she was there now.

She then turned to face her sisters, with red teary eyes. "Thank you," she told them as her voice broke up. "Thank you so much for helping me find her."

They all nodded their heads.

"Family is everything," Yessy said, giving her a warm reassuring hug. "I'm just glad we got them all back, sis."

Once they got the young ones out of Pancho's dungeon, going back up the stairs with the dogs bringing up the rear, they all saw Macho and Tool standing next to Pancho, who was on the floor, bleeding and trembling in fear.

Chloe's cousin saw him and in a fit of rage, ran on him and delivered a field of goal kicks to his jaw.

"Bitch! Nenda kuzimu!" she screamed, telling him to go to hell.

Chloe pulled her cousin away from him and out of the room. The women followed, each of them casting scowls at him as they passed by him. G-Baby and Felicia paused at Macho's side.

"P, Gabi, FeFe, y'all can go help Chloe. Me, bae and my brother got this bitch ass nigga from here," Macho said. Without a word, the three headed off to assist the Afro-Brit with the young ladies, leaving Tool, Macho and Yessy alone with the human-sex trafficker.

Yessy stood at her man's side and waited.

I don't think they like you very much, and neither do I," Macho said.

Yessy, with her knife out again, glared at Pancho. She visualized cutting his cock off and stuffing it into his mouth.

"Amor," Macho called to his woman.

She looked and saw her man was looking at her. "Yeah?"

"Grab that nail gun off the tool rack over there," he told her, as he put his gun in his holster.

Pancho watched the Nuyorican do as her boyfriend told her. He immediately freaked out, knowing they weren't about to hang fix anything with it.

"W-wait! Hold up, Joe! You said you wouldn't kill me!"

"I know what I said, clown! I'm not gonna kill you," Macho told Pancho, then in a flash, he and Tool snatched Pancho up off the floor and slammed him face-first into the wall, using all of their muscle to hold Pancho up against it. "What I am gonna do is let ya' bitch ass see how it feels to get taken advantage of! Bae! Nail this bitch ass nigga!"

Yessy squeezed the trigger repeatedly. Pancho screamed like Mariah Carey as nail after nail slammed into his ass crack, penetrating him.

"Aaaaaaaaahhhhhhh! Nooooooo!" he cried, trying so hard to get free, but was unable to due to the exceedingly strong Dominericans holding him in place.

Yessy emptied the clip into Pancho's ass. When the gun clicked empty, Macho and Tool let him go. The three watched him drop to the ground and wail like a dying Tasmanian Devil. Curling up into the fetal position, he tried to cup his ass but was unable to because of all the nails sticking out of it.

"Aww." Yessy crouched down next to him. "Does it hurt? Do you think it hurts more or less than when the grown-ass men you cater to stick their dirty-ass dicks into those little girls' vaginas?"

Pancho shook with agony, whimpering and sniffling back tears. Yessy stood back up and dropped the nail gun, taking one of her Glocks out and pointing it at Pancho's head.

"Ahora, te vas a morir por lo que hiciste, *bitch*," she said, cocking her gun.

"Hold up!" Macho stepped up next to her with an idea in mind

Yessy raised an eyebrow. "Why?"

Macho grinned. "Because I just got a great idea. He's gonna go meet Heavy B."

Yessy gasped. "Ooooooh." She looked at Pancho and bursted out laughing. "That is *waaaay* worse than a bullet to the head. Hell, even gettin' ya dick blown off is better than havin' to deal with *him*."

Macho looked down as Pancho. "I'm curious. What reason do you have to snatch up young girls when you was gettin' plenty of money movin' coke out here?"

"I didn't take them, man! It was this guy from Milwaukee! He's been snuggling girls into the States from different countries for the last year! You won't be able to stop him. Nobody can!"

Macho chuckled. "Oh really? Does this unbeatable person have a name?"

"Th-they c-call him *El Demonio*!" Pancho quickly snitched.

"Really? The Demon, huh? What a coincidence." Macho mocked, looking at his woman.

"All I know is that he's a Latin King from the South side of Mil', man!"

Macho's eyebrows furrowed when he heard that. Yessy glanced at her man, already knowing what he was thinking

"Don't even think about it, Antonio. It's over with after *this*. Mission accomplished," she declared.

Macho ignored her she focused on Pancho. "My homie is a King from out there."

Yessy shook her head at her man. "Eso maldito gordo no es tu fucking pana," she snapped.

He shook his head at her. "This is most definitely not the time to be airing out your problems with another individual. The task at hand is right here. Focus," he told her.

Yessy groaned in frustration but did as he had told her.

Pancho looked at Macho. "Your b-boy's a King from there, then y-y-you c-can call him and find out!" he said, trying to use that to his advantage. "Just l-l-let me go bro! Please! It hurts! I need a doctor!"

Macho and Yessy both shook their heads in disgust at him.

"Says all the little girls that happen to fall into the hands of dirty sleaze balls like you," Yessy said, wanting to pop Pancho so badly.

Pancho started getting delirious. "Wh-what more do you w-want from me?"

"We'll let Heavy B decide, bitch," said Macho.

Yessy then produced a plastic capped syringe from her sweatpants' pocket. She uncapped it and jabbed it into his neck, pushing the plunger down, injecting him with a very strong concoction that sent him to la-la land in mere seconds.

He and his brother then grabbed Pancho and dragged him out, with the Nuyorican behind them, gripping her automatic Glock in her hands.

Standing amongst the others, G-Baby, Felicia, and Perry watched Chloe speak to the young Nigerian girls in Swahili, assuring them that they were all safe. G-Baby could only imagine the things they'd been through in the time they'd been in Pancho's hands.

When Chloe gained their trust, City Cee, Dee, Lacey, G-Baby and Felicia all helped get the young ladies out of the building and into two Mercedes Sprinters that idled outside of the dock. The armed Jamaicans that were driving took off then, getting them out of there.

They went back inside when the Sprinters were gone. G-Baby went into the trailer and grabbed a big cardboard box out of it. She brought it out into the main area of Pancho's dock, setting it down in the middle of the warehouse floor.

The Ecuadorians watched, wondering what was inside the boxes, since they knew there was no cocaine inside of the trailer.

A few minutes later, Macho, Tool and Yessy came from Pancho's office, dragging the unconscious Ecuadorian behind them. Bringing up the rear was Yessy, with the dogs. Pancho's men gasped and started panicking amongst themselves, seeing their boss nearly naked, bleeding profusely from his ass.

Glancing at Macho, G-Baby suddenly felt those butterflies in her stomach that she just couldn't understand why she was having. She just could not stop staring at him.

"Gabi!" Felicia elbowed her in her side.

"Ow! Bitch! What the fuck is wrong with you?" G-Baby snapped, taking her eyes off Macho.

"Why are you starin' at him like that?" Felicia asked. "We on business! Get it the fuck together!"

G-Baby opened her mouth to speak when Yessy hollered to them.

"Ladies! Let's get up outta here! Mission accomplished!"

G-Baby ignored Felicia, then she pointed her shotgun at one of the men's legs. The others followed suit.

"No! Wait!" one of the men pleaded.

G-Baby, Felicia, and the others all shot every single one of the remaining made men in their legs, immobilizing them. Then without wasting another minute, they left out, leaving the screaming crying Ecuadorians on the bloody ground.

Yessinia

Macho and Tool dragged Pancho out of the building. The Sprinters with the young ones were gone, already en route to get the girls to safety. Idling next to the semi-truck that Yessy had driven there, was an older dark-colored Chevy Suburban that the SCM had arrived in.

Yessy and the dogs followed G-Baby towards where Macho's old creepy black 1985 Peterbilt 359 Extended Hood sat. The insanely powerful engine under the long stacks. The old Pete had been dubbed El Viejo, by Macho and his older brother. The way the classic rig shook and roared whenever its 1,400 horsepower Caterpillar engine was started up, made them think of a cranky Ol' Man that had been woken up out of his sleep. From the outside, El Viejo looked like just an old truck that a psychotic trucker would drive, but inside, Macho and his older brother had fixed the back and the flat-top-style sleeper berth with the luxuries of new Bentley Mulsanne.

***

Yessy and G-Baby got the dogs into El Viejo, then went into the luxurious box-shaped sixty-three-inch sleeper. G-Baby opened up what was called a "whore-door." Macho and

Tool handed Pancho to them through the windowless door that was in the side of the sleeper.

They stuffed Pancho down into a trap-spot under the bed, closed it and locked it. G-Baby and the dogs hopped onto the soft cool-gel bed, topped with Italian linen sheets and a Gucci blanket and got comfortable. Yessy got behind the wheel, closed the door and looked in the mirror. She saw her man.

Tool ran up along the passenger's side and hopped up into the cab, going back into the sleeper and joining G-Baby, Chloe, Taranda, and the dogs. Yessy clutched the eighteen-speed transmission into first gear as she simultaneously reached out to the dashboard to push in the tractor and the trailer's air-brake parking brake knobs to release the brakes. Letting off the clutch and the brake pedal, El Viejo started rolling forward. She pulled up from the dock and stopped so Macho could close and secure the trailer's doors. Putting the brakes on the shifter back into neutral, Yessy moved over to the passenger's seat as Macho ran up alongside the Pete's driver's side, opened the door and jumped up inside behind the wheel.

"Alrighty then, love," Macho said to his woman as he clutched into gear, released the brakes, and then started rolling towards the exit. "Let's make it rain creeps!"

"Yessir!" she replied, holding a little remote in her hand.

Macho carefully navigated the flooded pathway. His people in the 'Burban rolled behind him. He reached Kedzie Avenue and made a wide right turn out and hit it, banging gears like a pro, putting the pedal to the metal. The engine roared loudly every time he up-shifted. Flames spit out of the exhaust stacks, shooting nearly three feet above the rig. Yessy pointed the remote out of the window. She pressed the only button that was on it…

BOOOOM!

The bombs that were inside of the cardboard boxes that she and G-Baby had built detonated. Multiple explosions went off, ultimately leveling the entire building. Massive balls of fire went up into the pitch-black sky. The found rocked like an earthquake was hitting Chicago, waking up nearly all of the residents of Little Village.

"Wooooooo! Yeeeaaah, biiiitch!" Yessy shouted, as the building burned away any evidence of any of them ever being there. "Burn in hell, you fucking creeps!"

Everybody laughed at the turnt-up Nuyorican goddess. Everyone knew that Yessy loved actions, just as much as her man did.

Yessy chuckled at her own self as be reached out to the Kenwood pop-out head unit and put the music on, turning Chief Keef's "MONSTERS," featuring Lil' Reese.

"Aye!" Macho said to his woman. "What is you doin? You know the rules when we in Ol' Man, bae."

"Oh…I forgot," Yessy said, remembering the O.G. shit only rule Macho had whenever they were in El Viejo. She reached out the head unit and changed the music. Seconds later, Macho's favorite ol' school Hip Hop cut, KRS-One's "Step Into A World (Rapture's Delight)" came on and started pounding from the woofers.

Macho smiled. "Now that's what I'm talkin' about," he said, then got into cruise mode, nodding his head and rapping along with the ol' school Hip Hop cut.

Yessy shook her head and laughed at him.

Chapter 3

Just over an hour later, Macho got off of Highway Route 41, up in Lake County. He turned onto Wadsworth Road and shot east, arriving in Beach Park about ten minutes later. A minute after crossing over Green Bay, the entrance to his three-acre commercial yard came up. He turned into Numero Uno Transport, Macho's self-made multi-million-dollar trucking company with a big fleet of custom painted and chromed out semi-trucks. He rolled down the path road inside and saw the two Sprinters there. Posted up outside of them were those that had taken the young girls from hell, and took them to Chicago, where the Valdez family's matriarch had luxurious condominiums ready to accommodate them for a while.

Also, there were six black Hummer H2s and an ol' school two-door Mercedes SL560. The mob of Rastas that stood posted by the Hummers were part of the Valdez family's fearless Caribbean army, led by the older dread-head that was leaning against the Benz.

City pulled the Suburban around Macho and parked by the Hummers. Macho pulled his rig up and parked a few feet away from the ol' school SL, then he and the ladies and the dogs got out.

"Dere go me shottaz!" shouted the Jamaican, relieved to see his play nephews and the ladies were all safe.

He was a Kingston-born dreadhead who had been an essential part of the Valdez family since the three ol' heads that had built the multi-billion-dollar empire off Grade-A cocaine got their start, back in the seventies.

Jamaica was a little shorter than Macho, with light skin, and long thick dreads that were infused with gray hairs, and a thick scruffy beard. He was in his late fifties and had been the best friend of Macho's great uncle Diego, since Diego and his two older brothers, Juanito, and the deceased Pedro had begun building their massive multi-billion-dollar cocaine empire. He was fearless and devoted to the family, as they were for him and his actual family. Jamaica and Diego had been down together since they were kids, and had hopped from island to island, fighting in underground tournaments that were very popular. They had become a beast with their hands. By the time they were eighteen years of age, their names rang bells over Central and South America.

"Tio!" Macho shouted, excited to see his play uncle up and dapping him up. "Wha' gwan, rude bwoi!"

"Not a ting, tiguerre. Me and me bruddas woulda' andled dat for ya', but me know 'dis was personal for ya," Jamaica told him, as he embraced his oldest nephew.

Macho chuckled as Yessy came to his side. Jamaica gave her an uncle-like hug.

"How ya doin', Yessinia? Ya good, little mama?" he asked her.

Jamaica smiled at the two. To him and everyone else, Macho and Yessy were the epitome of a perfect couple. So many people wished they had the love and friendship the two had.

"It's a good 'ting ya got 'dem connections. Me know it wasn't easy to be able to find out where 'de blood-clot muddafuckaz would keep 'de young 'gyals. Me proud of you all," he told them, as G-Baby stepped up and received a warm hug from him as well. "And how about you, Chi-Town Gorilla Mama?" he asked her. "Ya good out here?"

G-Baby nodded. "As good as I can be livin' in a world full of fucked up people who don't realize that without women, there'd be no humans. I can't figure out why so many people subject women, especially young girls, to such fucked up situations?"

"Because they all some creepy-ass bitches, Gabi," Tool chimed in, hating it with a passion that so many men, and even other women, got down on ladies like it was actually okay to do. "I wish I could say that one day it'll change, but it won't."

"Well, we just gon' keep murkin' every bitch ass nigga that thinks it's' okay to be evil towards women," said Macho.

"And me and me goons are 'wit ya til' de wheels fall off, tiguere," Jamaica stated with serious eyes that told no lie.

***

Macho and Tool had the half-million that Pancho had paid for his re-up, plus another two million, sent to the young girls. But along with it, unbeknownst to the girls, Macho had not only paid all of their tuitions in full. While he and his woman were getting a location on them, along with housing and everything else they'd need money for to live comfortably while in school, he had reached out to his grandfather and grandmother, asking for their assistance so that if the girls wanted to stay in the states when they were done with school, they could, and for assistance getting all their families to the U.S.

Altogether, each girl received two hundred and seventy-five thousand in cash, free education, and would have a home with bills and utilities paid and full citizenship for them and their parents.

Having grown up in dilapidated areas of their country, living in shacks without running water, or anything else that even broke Americans had, he and his brother knew that the girls would be astounded. Macho and his brother were happy to be able to do something like that for them. They knew that the girls and their families would be good, but he was saddened by the very real fact that they were going back to some seriously fucked up living conditions. Doing good deeds was something the two Steel City Mafia brothers loved to do with their wealth. Helping people that needed it was something that allowed them to sleep great every single night.

***

Macho, Tool, Yessy, and G-Baby thanked their crew for helping out. Jamaica asked where Pancho was. Macho led the man towards El Viejo, hopped up inside and retrieved Pancho from the compartment under the bed. Pancho was beginning to stir awake as Macho jumped back out of the cab. He dropped Pancho on the ground. Pancho whimpered when he hit the pavement.

CRACK!

Jamaica kicked him square in the face. "Shut 'de fuck up, beetch!" he spat.

He called two of his goons to grab the son of a bitch and take him to one of the Hummers.

"Catch 'ya all latta', me family," Jamaica said to Macho, Yessy, Tool, and G-Baby.

His men hopped into their Hummers and pulled off. Jamaica hopped into his Benz and followed to take Pancho to the private airport around the corner, to where Macho's private Gulfstream G650 awaited to whisk the sex trafficker to his meeting with the family's most ruthless executioner.

City rolled over after the Rastas had left. Felicia hopped into the Suburban and joined her man in the back, drawing a curled lip-look from Lacey. Chloe thanked Macho and Tool's people emphatically for helping her get her cousin back. They all nodded their heads, making plans to link back up in Pittsburgh. City pulled off to head to the private airport where another private jet awaited to whisk them back to their homeland.

Todd dapped his brother up, hugged Yessy, G-Baby, Chloe, and Taranda, before going to and hopping in his sleek black 2015 Autobiography-edition Range Rover Supercharged and dipping ass as well.

Macho rode the ladies and the dogs over to where Yessy's exclusive matte-black Mercedes Benz G63 AMG sat in the centered parking lot, which was filled with foreigners and ol' schools belonging to the drivers of Numero Uno Transport. Yessy's G-Wagon was a special-order Brabus- edition 4x4 Squared model, sitting up on twenty-four-inch Modulare Monobocks, with big red brake calipers visible through the rims. Macho had it built in Germany, there were no other G63 4x4 Squared G-Wagons anywhere else on earth.

Next to it was Chloe's brilliant Alpine white BMW M760i xDrive, sitting on chromed Forgiato deuces tinted all the way around.

The woman and the dogs got out of El Viejo. Chloe and Taranda bid Yessy and G-Baby adieu, before hopping into the Beemer and parting ways.

Macho headed over to where he had a diesel fuel pump station at the rear of his yard. He parked at one, cut the engine off, and got out to fill.

At the driver's side of the tank, Macho leaned against the old rig, silently thanking the Man above for allowing him and his people to get Chloe's cousin back, along with the others. His phone started ringing a second later, bringing him out of his thoughts.

Macho left the pump nozzle in the spout of the fuel tank, climbed up into the cab and grabbed his phone off of the phone holder clip in the dashboard. He saw it was his big cousin Danny and immediately answered it.

"Yeeeeooooo, tigueraasooooo!" Macho shouted excitedly for the call from his cuz.

He was always happy to hear from the man that had practically raised him and his brother after the malicious murder of their father, and the death of their mother.

"What up, lil' cutty? How was that party, yo? I heard that shit was lit!" said Danny, in his baritone voice.

"Aww, maaan, cuzzo! Yo, niggaz had a muhfuckin' blast, 'yah mean? On the Homiez, cuz that shit was off the mutherfuckin' chain!"

Danny chuckled. "Good. I'm happy y'all had fun, yo."

Macho then brought up what Pancho had told him when his time had come to punch out.

"Aye, dude that we threw the party for told me a nigga they supposedly call El Demonio, be the one gettin' them party props that were there. You ever heard of him?"

"Negative."

"I was thinkin' about hittin' up Narco, since he's a ki—"

"Nigga, heeeell naw! Don't even bring dude into it! Fuck that snake-ass nigga, lil' cutty!" said Danny.

"But cuz, I'm sayin', he could—"

"Tonio! No! Listen to what I am sayin'! Nooooooo! N-motherfuking-o, nigga! Oiste, cabrón?"

Macho groaned in frustration. Everyone hated his homie Narco. For the life of him, he couldn't understand why. The man had saved his life more than once, had helped assist in getting the leader of a rival cartel that had been trying to kill his little cousin Javi, and he had hand delivered a clown into his and his family's hands, after he had been marked for death by Macho's younger cousin Xavier for beating his chick up, who coincidentally had been the guys baby mama, and had been terrorizing her and their young daughter. The guy had even somehow gotten Macho's younger cousin Evelyn to go against the family and take coke from their massive supply, and she just gave it to the guy. Macho was bewildered by how his own family could despise someone that did all that, just to lend a helping hand.

"Cuzzo, come on, man!" Macho began to argue. "Why not use logic with this? Narco is a king from up that way, and he has rank and can find anyone! Why not let me reach out to him and get him on it for find out who dude is?"

"Because I fuckin' said so, lil nigga! Don't question what I say, Tonio!" Dany snapped. "Fuck that snake-ass bitch! Why the fuck do you still rock with dude, man? Does it not mean anything to you that not one person in your circle likes him?"

"They don't know Narco like I do, cuz!" Macho continued.

"No me importa un carajo, cabrón! Que se vaya para carajo ese culebra!" Danny yelled, "On 'errrthang I love, Tonio. On Tommy, rest in peace, if you bring dude into the biz, I'm putting Tool on yo ass and you know ya' brother gon' get on that real quick about the fat dick eater motherfucker! Try me!"

Macho was taken aback by Danny's explosion. It wasn't often Danny got pissed off but when he did, it was worse than the storm that had just wreaked havoc over Chicago.

"Cono, cuz! Relax! Get off the gas pedal!" Macho said as he peeped his woman's G-Wagon rolling towards him. "Y'all be trippin' whenever y'all hear his name. I don't get it. He dun' saved my life twice!"

"He's the fuckin' reason ya' life was in danger in the first place, cabrón!" Danny shot back angrily. "Tonio! Use yo' muthafuckin' head! Dude is a snake! Wake the fuck up and smell the Folgers in ya cup, lil' cutty!"

"I am, cuz! Look at what Narco did for us! He helped us get closer to Victor Gomez's bitch ass, and he put that bitch ass nigga Stacks in our hands! Narco is not a snake!" Macho replied back, refusing to back down. "I am usin' my head! He's a king from Milwaukee! If this so-called El Demonio is, too, then why shouldn't I at least ask bro if he knows who the guy is? Or if he's even ever heard of him?"

"Because if you involve him in family business, I'm puttin' Tool on ya' ass! That's why!" Danny declared.

Macho shook his head and changed the topic.

"You cool, though? You need anything?"

Surprisingly, Danny started laughing. "Naw, lil cuz."

"Okay. I know you're a billionaire, but everybody needs somethin', cutty."

Danny chuckled. "What could I possibly need, besides freedom? Check it, yo, I own the commissary vendors that supply sixteen prisons across the United States, and I own the only telecommunications system that can compete with Securus and GTL. ChaCha has been keeping PJ&D running perfectly since I have been locked up. I still have my mother and all y'all lil' knuckleheads. I got air in my lungs, and my mind. I can't ask for nothin' else, Tonio, 'yah mean?"

Macho agreed. "I feel you."

"Do you realize that even being locked up, us that are in prison live like kings compared to so many other countries in the world? There are so many third-world countries that don't even have running water that they can drink. The food one gets in prison is ten times better than what the people in dilapidated neighborhoods in Africa and so many cities in Latin America get, if they get anything to eat at all! Yo, we are literally living better than half the world, in prison! Muhfuckaz that are in and complain about conditions, number one, they haven't been to Stateville NRC."

Macho busted out laughing. "Homiez, cuz! Yooo, on 'errthang that place is fucked up!" he shouted, remembering having gone through the Northern Receiving Center for maximum security prison of the Illinois Department of Corrections, down in Joliet, Illinois. There it was twenty-four-hour lockdown, two showers a week, tiny Lunchables-size food trays, toilets that flushed on timers, and outdoor rec every few days inside what were like dog kennels. The "dog kennels" were without bathrooms since whenever you went outside, you were stuck for hours until the COs come to let everyone back into their disgusting cells.

Danny continued. "Number two, again, even being inside we live way better qualities of life compared to those living in countries that have no bare necessities, and with governments that do everything to take from them and keep them living in what is actually worse than poverty. I've done a lot of good things in my life, lil' cuz, but I've also done a lot of bad things."

"Bad things to bad people," Macho added, to make a point as the fuel pump stopped from the tank being full.

"Be that as it may," Danny continued. "Two wrongs don't make a right."

"Okay, you been readin' them philosophy books again, uh?" Macho asked, as he screwed the fuel tank cap back on and went to go climb over the frame behind El Viejo's sleeper berth and the front of the trailer.

Laughing again, Danny replied, "No, but you should know, since you did a bid, that bein' in prison makes a lot of us wonder about everything. Many of us want to find out who we are and why we were put on earth. Makes us wanna' find out about those that came before us. Learning about how truly fucked up the times were back in the early days for our ancestors, makes you really appreciate life as we know it today, and even if a muhfucka had to rub out a few clownz, you always think about what you could've did differently, 'yah mean? It's the difference between movin' like Dr. King, being peaceful but still bein' fearless like Malcolm X, wit that 'If you hit me, I'ma hit you back' type of mindset."

"Shheeeeeeeeeeeeeittt! If anybody lays a hand on me or mines, I'm turnin' them into Rottweiler and Pitbull food. Homiez, cuz!" Macho declared, as he unscrewed the cap to the passenger's tank and inserted the nozzle.

Danny laughed again. "You sound like ChaCha, Yessy, and Michelle, always tryna feed people to the dogs. They gon' get fat fuckin' round with y'all mutherfuckers, yo."

Macho busted out laughing at his cousin.

Chapter 4

Yessinia

Getting behind the wheel of her exclusive G-Wagon, Yessy push-started the engine and 700-horsepower barked to life out of the twin sport tuned exhaust pipes. The twin-turbo Brabus built V8 sounded so mean and powerful. It gave Yessy goosebumps every time she started it up.

Sitting in the front passenger's seat, Maliante panted, tongue hanging out of his mouth as his owner, G-Baby sat in back with Dreams, stroking behind her ears, yawning from how tired she was.

"Stop it, Gabriella," Yessy told her, as she pulled out her iPhone when it buzzed in her pocket.

G-Baby looked up at her. "Stop what?"

Yessy opened the email sent to her by one of the drivers, read it, and sent up a fast reply.

"Yawning. It's contagious," she joked, then yawned herself as she put her G-Wagon into drive and started rolling towards the fuel station.

G-Baby twisted her lips up. "Can't help it. I'm tired as hell, man," she replied back, leaning her head back against the headrest and closing her eyes for a minute. Yessy chuckled as she came to a stop next to the edge of the fuel pump station, parking closest to El Viejo's passenger's side. Looking at her man, Yessy smiled to herself. She adored him to no end. To the current day, she could never truly describe how he made her feel. Love just didn't seem to capture it all.

He was her everything, and she knew that she was his everything.

The twenty-seven-year-old was born and raised in Pittsburgh, Pennsylvania. He was the product of a major Dominican cocaine drug lord, and a corporate smart Puerto Rican businesswoman. Macho was raised in Homewood, of Allegheny County, in an all-African American neighborhood. Yessy loved how he was the perfect mix of Latino and African. Her being from New York, being Afro-Latino was a thing to be proud of and shout from the rooftops. He was aware of his existence and never once denied anything about his people's history.

He was the third oldest in the Steel City Mafia. Yessy found their clique intriguing. They were all raised the same by their fathers, taught how to be street smart, how to work hard for what they got, and how to understand that just because one was born into money did not make them rich, until they learned how to get it on their own.

The way he lived life on a daily basis was admirable to Yessy. He was richer than most rich people but still got up every day and was on business, getting it like he still hadn't got it. Most of the time, what she saw was when someone got rich, the hunger for more died, and they no longer had the fire inside of them. Macho was different from that. To her, it seemed like the more money he made, the more ambitious he got. He constantly made investments that were smart and calculated, and he also gave tons of money away, just to see someone reach for the stars and shine like one.

Macho's family being heavies in the trucking world was something Yessy hadn't been used to seeing. She grew up seeing many business owners that were people of color, back in her childhood days in the Bronx, but the business that Macho's family was involved in, and killing it, was like seeing Jay-Z, Dame Dash, Rick Ross, Lil' Wayne, and all the other mega-moguls out there still in the streets and getting it with their own hands, instead of hiring people to do their work for them. Macho, his brother, and their cousins all owned trucking companies, but also had their hands in many other business ventures that expanded their portfolios. Should they ever actually not want to work, their money would still flow in like a summer breeze through an open window.

Yessy was so drawn to her man. His selflessness was unbelievable. He literally was the type of guy to give someone a million dollars to start a business and not want a dime in return. Their being successful was payment enough for him. Add in the billion-dollar inheritance that he and his brother split into two, when their father was murdered, giving away money was damn near sport for Macho and his brother.

His good looks were the other major factor in how insanely drawn to him she was. His rich creamy golden-brown skin tone, his amazingly sculptured two-hundred-sixty-pound frame, all his tattoos, his long soft hair, strong face, and more than anything else, his dreamy bluish-gray eyes, truly azure in color, which hypnotized her every time his gaze fell upon her. They always got her engine running.

G-Baby

She opened her eyes, and they landed right onto him. She couldn't help but gaze at the incredibly handsome Dominerican, as he finished filling the passenger's side fuel tank of the old Peterbilt. The song "So Gone" by Monica suddenly started playing in her head. She just could not take her eyes off him. He was the shit and piss in her eyes. She looked over at the caramel-complexioned Nuyorican. G-Baby admired her best friend to no end. She found Yessy to be one of the most beautiful ever, with her flawless skin tone, her long black silky hair, her tattoos, and her voluptuous physique. G-Baby was attracted to women, and had no problem sexing one, but she hadn't ever pictured herself playing bumper cars with her sis. What she found funny about the twenty-six-year-old, was how she really did resemble Gina Rodriquez, a Puerto Rican actress from Chicago, best known for her role in the TV show *Jane The Virgin,* like everyone always said she did. She even had freckles like the actress, but Yessy was just taller and waaay thicker.

G-Baby and Yessy had so much in common, which was why they were so tight. They were just months apart in age, close to the same height, thick and gorgeous, military trained, and they were both from wild Puerto Rican neighborhoods.

G-Baby was from down in Chicago's Humboldt Park neighborhood, and Yessy was from The Bronx's Morrisania Projects, where the famous rapper Fat Joe came up. They were both victims of broken homes.

G-Baby was sent up to Waukegan to live with her auntie after contact fights between her and her younger sister, due to them hanging with two different Latino gangs that had been on the streets.

Yessy and her younger brother had made the trek to their mother's mom in Waukegan, after their dope fiend mother overdosed on heroin, leaving them by themselves. Yessy's father, and her brother's father, were non-existent in their lives, so all they had was their mother, and as G-Baby and Yessy had gotten tight back when they were in school, she'd gathered that a lot of things had happened to Yessy that she never wanted to speak on,

After they completed their primary education, G-Baby and Yessy decided that they wanted to do something crazy. By then, Macho and Yessy were deeply involved and deeply in love. When they went to him and said they were going to join the army, they'd both expected him to flip out and say what everyone else said about fighting for the white man, but he didn't. He supported any and every decision they made. They enlisted and chose to become truck drivers, mostly because of Macho's family. They ended up in Missouri's

Fort Leonard-Wood, where truck drivers were trained for Heavy Equipment Transportation units, and they instantly fell in love with it.

Over the years, they'd transported everything from ammunition explosives, food to Humvees, personnel carriers, and massive battlefield tanks. They'd even had to chance to go overseas. Though women weren't yet in front line units, they still had to be alert when transporting freight from seaports or airfields to the Forward Operating Bases. There were, though, plenty of times where they had to utilize the infantry training they had at the very beginning stages of their enlistment, and because of their tenacity and their bravery they excelled at whatever they did. Yessy's and G-Baby's names rang bells. During their time together in the service, they made many friends and connections in high places.

G-Baby had discharged from the service just a few weeks ago. She'd reached the rank of a Captain before she called it quits and was discharged with honors. Yessy, who had reached the rank of a major, was still active, but was due to be discharged in the upcoming weeks, and G-Baby prayed every day that what they'd been working on while they were both in would come to fruition. If it did, they were about to be seriously up and Macho would be beyond geeked about it.

Yessinia

"Gabriela Medina, if you don't stop staring at me, I'ma tell ya' girlfriend that you're fantasizing about me so she can beat cha' ass," Yessy told her home girl.

Yessy heard G-Baby suck her teeth. "Bitch, ain't nobody lookin' at you, and I do not have a girlfriend. Get it right."

Yessy busted out laughing as she saw her man take the fuel pump back to hang it up and hop back up into the old rig.

"So you and Nya ain't in a relationship?" asked Yessy, now looking at her.

"No! Hell naw, yo ass tweakin', sis!" G-Baby exclaimed.

"Am I?" Yessy twisted her lips up at G-Baby when El Viejo's engine started up.

G-Baby waved her home girl off. "I let the bitch eat me out once, and I ate hers. That doesn't make her my bitch, nor does it make me hers!"

Yessy nodded in agreement. "Facts, but she's gone over you. So, you might wanna' stop lettin' her taste ya poon-poon before she develops a fatal attraction."

G-Baby waved her off again then laid her head back against the headrest, closing her eyes. Yessy smiled, snickering to herself as she looked at the amazingly gorgeous twenty-six-year-old Chicagorilla. G-Baby was truly breathtaking. Her skin-tone was so closely similar to that of maple pancake syrup. She had such an exotic look to her, with eyes that were slightly slanted like an Asian's were.

G-Baby, at five foot eight inches tall, was just an inch shorter than her. They both loved flaunting their stuff, but they were humble women, living simply, despite the fact that they were rich as hell. They lived as honestly as they could, but when drama came to their doorstep, they went from beautiful ladies, to heartless gangstresses in the flash of an eye.

***

After Macho went and parked El Viejo just outside of Bay 2, Yessy watched him walk back to where the Ol' Man's air tank was mounted to the frame, just past the rear of the sleeper berth. When he opened the valve at the bottom of it and manually drained all the air out to expel any water or compressor oil that might have built up inside of it, which would affect the braking system. The loud hissing of the air caused the dogs to start barking. Yessy pulled Maliante to her and calmed him down, while G-Baby gave Dream's belly a rub. After all the air was drained, Yessy saw her man coming towards her window. She rolled it down and was surprised by a soft kiss on the lips, followed by the sexy smile that always got her engine running.

"Meet me in the office," he told her, then headed towards the office's main entrance door.

Yessy started grinning her ass off. She looked back at G-Baby, who was looking at her.

"So… I'll be right back," she said to her, then as if a fire had just been lit under her ass, Yessy jumped out of the G-Wagon and ran to catch up with her man, leaving G-Baby shaking her head, wishing that she too was invited to get some of that stroke game that she knew Macho had, judging by the way that when Yessy screamed and cried out in bliss, she was louder than a woman giving birth to twins at the same time.

Chapter 5

Macho

Macho stepped into his plush, presidential-looking office and turned on the lights. He went to the computer on his desk and turned the music on. T-Pain's "Studio Luv" came on, crooning from the surround sound speakers wirelessly linked to the computer.

Yessy entered the office less than a minute later, just as he dimmed the lights. She immediately rushed him, so hot and horny for him. Macho wrapped her up in his massive python-sized arms and kissed her hungrily, heating her up more and more. Yessy got so hot that she felt like she was going to burst into flames.

Somehow, Yessy managed to pull back. As she did, when her eyes locked on his, she started stripping naked. Macho followed her lead and got naked right with her. They gazed at each other's bodies, transfixed by what they saw and had loved for so long.

Macho was completely wowed by his woman's amazingly fit, yet curvaceous body. She had 36-DD cup breasts, a twenty-six-inch waist, and wide forty-six-inch hips, with so much ass that he could never resist putting his face between her plump cheeks every chance he got.

Yessy smiled seductively as she gazed at him. "ChaCho, papi," she said, biting her lip as she grew so aroused. "Me encanta lo que veo," she added, eyeing his thick ten-inch, two-toned cock, licking her lips in anticipation of it being deep down her throat. "Dios Mio, bebe, you are so blessed," said Yessy, taking it into her hand and giving it a little squeeze.

"I am blessed." Macho leaned in and kissed her lips. "Blessed to have you in my life."

Yessy's heart started beating a mile a minute. His words always got her. Always so heartfelt and sincere. The way he loved her, and talked to her was like that of a Hallmark love movie.

"Oh, my God, Antonio. You are so sweet!"

"I bet you're sweeter," he replied, then running his hands down her sides, to her thick thighs and to her plump ass, he squeezed it and picked her up. "Let's see how many licks it takes to get you trembling before you cum all in my face."

Picking her up, Macho put his woman on his desk, pulled her close to the edge. He kissed her softly, passionately, then he licked his way down to her chest. Yessy moaned, throwing her head back when she took one of her breasts into his mouth. Her breathing grew labored. She felt like she was bathing in molten lava.

Macho sucked on her right breast, then her left. She was so wet, but he knew she could get even wetter. He kissed down to her flat stomach. He laid her back as he got close to her womanhood, then bypassed it to kiss down her thighs, to her legs, then her feet.

He kissed them both and sucked on her toes. Yessy was seeing stars. She appreciated how there were not limits to what her man wouldn't do to please her. His display of love and affection was never hindered by anything, and she went hard to reciprocate her love back to him.

After he licked his way back up, he planted soft kisses on the insides of her thick thighs. Yessy moaned, feeling his lips so close to her throbbing center. Just then, Twista's "Wetter," featuring Ericka Shavon came on.

Yessy felt like her head was about to explode. And he hadn't even slid up inside of her yet. She felt him at her love button, pushing the hood to her clit up. The second she felt him French kissing her clit, hew whole body arched up from the unbelievable amount of pleasure. She cried out his name as her whole body responded in ways that she just couldn't understand.

"Antonio! Oooo! Cono! ¡Mamame la chocha, papi! ¡Asi, papi!" she cried out, begging for him to keep going.

He dined on her, sucking and slurping her up like she was the most delicious meal. Her scent, her flavor, and the way she moaned and screamed while he ate her up made Macho go harder on her. He loved pleasing his woman. The freaky things he did to her gave her the most intense orgasms ever.

"Fuck!" she shouted, her body quivering as she felt herself so close to cumming so hard.

Macho kept sucking her clit and added two fingers inside of her to stimulate her enough to where she craved penetration. Ten seconds later, Yessy came so hard that she squirted all over his face. She drenched him like she had a Super Soaker inside of her.

"¡Cono!" she cursed, laying limp on the desk, breathing hard and fast to refill her depleted lungs with air. "You and those freaking lips and tongue! Goddammit, Antonio! My legs are numb!"

Macho busted out laughing. "You tapped out?" he asked in a taunting way.

Yessy looked at him. "You got me fucked up, yo," she replied.

In a flash, Yessy was up off the desk and down on her knees before him. Macho leaned against his desk, groaning out in sheer bliss as his woman took his throbbing cock into her mouth. She took him to the back of her throat with ease. She started humming. The vibration tickled his balls so much that he almost screamed from the sensation.

"¡Maldito!" he cursed, as Yessy released him from her throat, to where the bulbous tip of his dick was between her lips. She sucked hard on it. When she released it, it made a popping sound.

"Te gusta, papi?" she asked him as she looked up. She spit on his dick and used one hand to jerk his shaft. "Te gusta la forma que te lo mamés?"

"Yes! Shit!" he groaned gutturally as her hand stroked him. "Mamamelo este cabrón, bebe!"

Yessy took him back into her mouth and pleased him until he busted his nut a few minutes later. She let him fill her mouth up with hot globs, then she let it dribble down onto her chest.

"Mmmmm, papi, it tastes so good," she purred, after swallowing the rest of his jizz.

Still horny and dying to slide up in her wetness, Macho pulled her up from her knees pulling her to him.

"You are so strong, papi." Yessy was turned on by Macho's raw strength.

"You make me strong, love, pero ahora mismo, esta chocha jugosa, me la voy a batear bien rico hasta que vienes bien duro," he told her, ready to beat the pussy up.

He spun her around, made her grab the desk. Macho dropped down behind her and buried his face in the crack of her ass. He kissed and licked all up and down, swirling his tongue around her asshole. Yessy squealed in delight, rising up on her tippy toes when his tongue entered her puckered chute. She loved how freaky her man was. She loved how there was nothing he wouldn't do to turn her on and make her cum. Behind closed doors, they both pleased each other to no end, but even in public, they were known to get nasty with each other.

After he made her soak his face again. Macho stood up and slid himself into her wetness. Leaning down so that her face nearly lay on the desk's surface. Yessy hissed as his length stretched her tight walls out. The sting quickly turned into pleasure as he long stroked the pussy, going so deep that Yessy swore she could feel it up in her chest.

"Aay! Aay! Papi! Yeeess! Fuck me! Oh, God yeeess!"

Macho gripped her wide hips and started pounding her as hard as he could. He jack-hammered her wet-wet like he was trying to break up a concrete sidewalk. Yessy came within minutes, squirting all over his dick.

The next thing Macho knew, he found himself in his comfortable high-back chair behind his desk. His woman, on top of him, rode his stiff cock like she was a jockey, and he was her champion racehorse.

"Fuck! Wooo! Ride this dick, baby! Ride this muhfucka!" he shouted.

Yessy moved to the beat of Verse Simmonds' "Boo Thang," featuring Kelly Rowland and Yo Gotti. She looked down into his eyes and concentrated on him. She made love to him, with more than just her body.

Looking up at her, Macho couldn't get over how beautiful his woman was. She was amazing. He looked up into her eyes. Their eyes stayed locked on each other's, their hearts pounding on the same note. Yessy leaned down and cupping his face between her hands, she kissed him while still keeping her rhythm. She sat back upright and threw her head back, screaming out in bliss as she brought them both closer to climaxing.

G-Baby

G-Baby listened through the door, hearing them going crazy inside. Even over the music, she heard Yessy crying out her man's name, and him groaning and cursing.

Her panties were drenched and she leaked down the insides of her thighs. Her nipples were hard, aching for his touch. She felt so hot that not even a cold shower would cool her off.

God, I need a man so fucking bad...or at least some dick...some good Macho dick, she thought, then she started laughing at herself.

Feeling a presence behind her, G-Baby turned around and saw the dogs a few feet behind her. Dreams and Maliante sat next to each other, staring at her with their heads tilted to the sides, trying to figure out what she was doing.

"Don't judge me," G-Baby told them, then she headed back towards the garage area to step outside, and attempt to cool off.

Chapter 6

Macho

"Woooo!" shouted Macho, laying on his back under his woman, in the middle of the office's floor, both of them sweating hard and breathing harder. Yessy started laughing at him, lifting her head up and looking down into his eyes.

"Good job, babe," she congratulated, before leaning down to plant a kiss on his lips. "I needed that."

"I aim to please. I think we should get dressed and head out, though. G-Baby probably wonderin' what we doin' in here 'n shit."

"Trust me, she most definitely knows."

"Next time, we should invite her to join us," Macho added with a grin.

"What?" his woman snapped, her smile disappeared, and a narrow-eyed glare replaced it.

"Oh, whoa, whoa, whoa…calmate, bae, I was just playin'," he capped, cursing inside of his head as he realized his woman would never entertain the idea of a threesome.

Yessy stayed sitting on top of him. She grabbed his wrists and pinned them down on the floor, making sure that he couldn't go anywhere while she said what she was about to tell him. "Te lo fucking juro por Dios, Antonio, si alguna vez permites que otra mujer te toque… otra vez, te voy a batear tu culo y esa puta yo voy a cortar en pedazos y se la alimento a Maliante y Dreams! ¡No estoy jugando contigo!"

Thinking back to what Danny had said, Macho busted out laughing at his woman, which made her even angrier.

"You, Michelle, and ChaCha need to stop feeding the dogs people, that's why they getting chubby now, yo."

"¡No me importa un carajo! Tu me escuchaste lo que dije, Antonio!"

"Yes, I heard you loud and clear, and I said before…I was just fucking playing!"

Yessy leaned down and put her forehead to his. "Who you yelling at?"

"The ceiling," Macho told her, immediately falling back.

She busted out laughing at him. "That's what I thought, nigga," she replied, then jumped up off of him. "Now let's get dressed and get home."

Yessy took her man's hand and helped him up off the floor. He wrapped her up in his bulky arms and kissed her until she came close to climaxing. When he pulled back, he looked down into her eyes and smiled.

"I love you, you crazy-ass pork chop."

Yessy laughed. "I love you too, you half-pork chop mutt motherfucker. I have one more thing to say though, before we leave."

"Okay?" Macho looked at her with puzzled brows.

"If you even think about bringing your punk bitch, so-called friend Narco into anything we are going to do to find El Demonio, you won't need to worry about Tool."

She got up and went to get her clothes. Macho got up and stood there for a minute watching his lady. His eyes went down to her phat juicy booty. An evil grin grew on his face. He snuck up behind her, just as Yessy bent over to pick up her underwear and…

SMACK!

"Aaaayyyy, motherfuckeeeerrrr!" she shouted from the sting, grabbing her ass cheeks and rubbing them. "Lo juro por Dios, Antonio! Te voy a batear el fucking culoooo!" she then yelled and rushed Macho, catching him before he could take off.

Yessy jumped on him and took him to the floor. She started flooding him, raining down punch after punch. Macho blocked his face from her furious fists with his forearms. He laughed his ass off at her, teasing and taunting her.

"Hahahahaha! I am Machoooo!" he shouted, taunting her. "Hear me roar! Rraaaaaaarrrr, muddafuckaaaaa!"

Leading her man out of the office, Yessy saw the lights on in the garage. Holding his hand, Yessy led Macho down the hallway that led to the garage's service area. Parked right on the other side of the entrance door in Bay 1 was Macho's prized 2007 Legacy Class edition Peterbilt 379 Extended Hood. Only a thousand of them were made.

The Legacy Class was customized to the max. The Pete gleamed like it was sitting on the showroom floor of a dealership. So much exterior chrome and stainless steel had been added to compliment the exclusive dark jade metallic paint job. The twenty-four-and-a-half-inch wheels were custom made to resemble blades and were topped with pointed lug nut covers. The high-gloss polish made them shine like new chrome. The rear-end had been stretched a little longer to give the truck a lowered hot-rod like stance.

Inside the cab and the seventy-inch stand-up style sleeper were decked out with dark jade and black alligator accenting, and wired up in both was a pavement-pounding sound system that made people's teeth rattle.

Yessy loved Macho's flashy Peterbilt. Everything about its style. Macho had made sure not a single thing on the truck was stock. Her favorite part of it was the low hanging straight edged drop windshield visor, that made the truck look furious, and the two huge ten-inch monster exhaust stacks, that when the engine was started up, the truck sounded furious. You could actually feel the powerful Caterpillar engine when it was on.

Everything done to the Legacy Class was well over six hundred and fifty thousand, but the monetary value of it meant nothing to Macho. Its value was more sentimental to him and his brother. They rebuilt her from the frame up, and then to give their mother the time of her life for the last few weeks of it, until cancer took her away, they had taken her on a road trip all over the country, attending truck shows, while hauling high-dollar freight. Cristina had loved the Legacy Class Pete, but more than that, she loved the time she got to spend with her sons. Their time together was a representation of when the three of them had no cares in the world, other than just being a loving family. There was nothing in life more meaningful than tha. So, Macho's Legacy Class was irreplaceable to him and had value beyond any of his possessions.

***

Finding G-Baby behind the wheel of the Legacy, with the dogs chillaxing next to the truck, Macho and Yessy beckoned to them and headed out of the garage, packing into Yessy's G-Wagon. She pulled off and headed north to Zion,

Minutes later, after passing through Green Bay Road and Route 173, Yessy arrived at the massive subdivision that Macho bought as bare land and had turned into his own neighborhood. Just over eighty luxurious two- and three-story houses sat on one hundred acres of land, on the quiet and peaceful outskirts of the Z.

She pulled up into the driveway of their big 4,600 square foot two-story, hitting the button to the built in two-car garage. They all hopped out and entered the garage where Macho's new shit, a Bentley Mulsanne sat next to Yessy's new black Mercedes S650 Maybach.

In between the two big body foreigners was G-Baby's blacked out Suzuki GSXR. Her crotch rocket gleamed under the light and looked powerful enough to take off without a rider on it.

***

Inside, G-Baby instantly went off to her side of the house. She had her own crib in the subdivision, but she barely went there. Neither of them liked being too far from each other. Living the life that they lived, the power of three was better than one.

"I am beyond tired," Macho said, as he and his woman headed to a custom designed lounge area with a recessed section in the middle, built with an oval-shaped lagoon in it. "Killin creep-ass sex traffickers is actually hard work."

Yessy chuckled as they arrived at the lagoon. In the murky waters four heads of baby caimans were just above the surface. They all turned and looked up at the humans, then the two furry four-legged creatures that were growling at them.

"They look hungry," said Yessy, looking at who she and Macho named Fats, Rex, Ladron, and Beef.

"Can't wait 'til they big enough to eat bitch ass niggaz that don't deserve to live."

He and Yessy went and got a bunch of feeder goldfish from the giant fish tank in their walk-in closet sized food pantry and fed the hungry mini gators. They watched with glee as the four mini gators snapped up thirty fish in less than a minute, as if they would never get the chance to eat again.

The dogs got bowls full of food, fresh water, and their automatic dog door to the backyard was unlocked so they could go out and come in as trained.

Heading up the stairs, Macho led his woman up to their bedroom. Macho yawned repeatedly, exhausted from such a long day. They entered the deluxe bedroom and were instantly relaxed from the soothing, Afro-Latino art and decor. It was their most favorite palace to be whenever they were at home, after a long hard day of chaos.

Wale's "Bad," featuring Tiara Thomas, played from the surround-sound speakers around in the massive master bedroom. The lights were dimmed low, and a fresh breeze blew through the wall of floor-to-ceiling windows that looked out over the massive backyard.

Laid back against his soft satin pillow, Macho responded to a few emails he'd received, requesting transport services, a few emails were from his drivers that had delivered their loads, before dropping everything and getting to the garage. Those emails included photos of signed bill of ladings, which were shipping papers. The documents had been signed by the supervisors of the companies the loads were delivered to. Macho used what was called factoring company to get paid whenever a load was confirmed delivered. The factoring people required proof of delivery, which was a simple photo of signed manifests. Once they had that, they would issue the amount agreed upon between the owner of the load and the shipper, minus the small fee they charged for their service. They then billed the owner of the load for the full amount, which was how they made their money, and were able to keep business with truckers and trucking companies.

There were seven loads that Macho forwarded to the factoring company. Each one was for over twenty thousand. After he finished with the factoring people, he went to a website and checked on the two custom builds that he had paid an arm and a leg to have created for his woman and G-Baby.

The pictures he saw of them in progress made a gigantic smile grow on his face. He loved what he saw, and he couldn't wait for the day that he could surprise them with the two beautiful rolling works of art.

***

"Baby?"

Looking towards the doorway to the bedroom, his eyes went wide with surprise when he saw her, standing in the doorway. She was posing provocatively in a sexy red lace L'Agent by Agent Provocateur bra and thong set, with red stilettos on her feet, and her hair down, looking wet like she had just gotten out of the shower.

"Well, damn!" he exclaimed at the very sight of her.

Yessy licked her sexy red lips "Whatcha doin'?" she asked in a flirtatiously innocent way.

"Visualizing myself kissin' all over you, then smackin' on the phat brown juicy booty while I'm hittin' it from the back."

Mmmmmmmmm… me encanta como suena eso, papi," she told him. "Pero yo tengo una sorpresa para ti."

"A surprise?" he asked her.

She nodded. "It's something I know you been wanting for a really really long time, too."

"What might that be?"

Yessy smiled so seductively at him. She stepped to the side, then seconds later, Macho's jaw dropped.

No…fucking…way…naw…heeeellll naw…I am not seeing this! *No*! *Uh-uh*! he thought, blinking his eyes and rubbing them swearing up and down that he was seeing things.

Standing next to his woman, was G-Baby, wearing the same sexy lace bra and thongs, pumps, red lipstick and her wet-looking hair hanging loosely as well.

"Us," Yessy said, taking G-Baby's hand and leading her towards the bed. "Giving all of us to you, papi."

Macho was stuck in shock as he watched the two thick beautiful Boricuas strut towards him. He was frozen in place, hypnotized and stuck in a trance at the same damn time.

"This is a dream," he told himself, as the song changed to Cassidy's "Get No Better," featuring Mashonda. "There is no way this is really happening."

"Oh, this is definitely happening, baby," Yessy said as she and G-Baby got to where he was. "The way you have always been so selfless and loving for all of us, you deserve this."

"Yeah," G-Baby said, with eyes full of liquid desire. "Te queremos mucho, Antonio. Estamos bien calientes y mojados para ti."

Hearing her tell him that they wanted him so badly, and that they were hot and wet for him, had Macho's dick ready to bust through his boxer briefs. His dick throbbed so much that it hurt.

He saw G-Baby's eyes fall down to where the tent in his Polos was. She licked her lips at the sight of it.

"Ay, chacho, papi. Dejame ver ese gran bicho," she told him and reached for his boxer briefs, pulling the waistline down.

Macho was still stuck. Yessy started giggling at him.

"You still don't believe this is happening, huh?" she asked as G-Baby yanked his Polos all the way down to his ankles and off, tossing them over her shoulders.

While she feasted her eyes on his thick two-toned pole, Macho shook his head.

"I'm dreaming…this is not real…you would never let another woman touch my dick."

"True…normally, I would chop the bitch's hand off and make her eat her fingers, but this isn't just another woman," Yessy told him. "This is now your bitch," she added.

G-Baby wrapped a hand around his dick and slowly started jerking his shaft.

Macho groaned from the feeling.

"Te gusta?" Yessy asked him.

He hissed, "Yessssss!"

"Y que sobre…esto?" she then asked him.

G-Baby started lowering her face down to his crotch. She opened her mouth wide and took his dick into her mouth.

"Ooohhhh, shhhhheeeeeeeeiiiiitt!" he groaned, feeling her warm and wet cave of a mouth envelop him. "Holy shit! Godddammmit… goddammmit… goddammit!"

Yessy put her hand on the back of G-Baby's head, and she started sucking her man's dick. Macho cursed and groaned, toes curling up, his back arching from the bliss. His eyes rolled in the back of his head when she deep throated his length like ten inches was nothing to her.

"You like how her mouth feels, baby?" Yessy asked.

"Yes! Yes! Hell, motherfucking yes! Shit!"

G-Baby spit his dick out and ran her tongue down his shaft. She went down to his nuts and kissed them, taking them into her mouth and sucking on them.

Macho's head was spinning around and around as G-Baby pleasured him. Yessy climbed up onto the bed and pushed him all the way onto his back. She climbed onto his face but turned away so that she was facing G-Baby.

Macho wasted no time in pleasing his woman. He reached up and grabbed ahold of her thick thighs and ate her pussy like it was his last meal. He could feel G-Baby sucking his dick again, while stroking his shaft with her hand. His dick pulsated in her mouth. He was damn near ready to bust his nut already.

"Ooohhh…Antonio! Yes!" Yessy moaned out as she started sliding her wetness back and forth on his face. "Mamemela, papi! Eat this pussy up! Shit!"

He continued pleasing her as G-Baby continued sucking him. Yessy bucked, kicked trembling and shook on his face. She leaked like a broken faucet in the projects. Minutes later, she cried out his name at the top of her lungs and came all over his face. She fell sideways, chest rising and falling fast as she tried to catch her breath.

"Fuck!" she cursed, lying next to her man. "Goddammit, Antonio! What the fuck?"

G-Baby spit his dick out, then refusing to let it go, she moved up his body mounting him so she could ride on it. He looked up into her eyes and saw the twinkle in them. She licked her lips again as she positioned herself on top of his cock.

She slid down on it. Macho cursed from the feeling of her tight wet pussy swallowing all of his dick, down to his balls.

"Fuck! Finally!" he shouted.

"This what you've been wanting?" G-Baby asked, just as Twista's "Make A Movie," featuring Chris Brown started playing.

"Yes! Yes! I been wantin' this pussy for years!"

"Mmmmmmm shit!" she moaned as his size stretched her walls out. "You c-c-could've had it if you would've told me, Antonio," she stammered.

Macho sat up and kissed on G-Baby's breast while she gyrated her hips, riding his joint like she was dancing. She moaned and cried out in sheer bliss. Pushing him back down, G-Baby grabbed his pectorals and squeezed. Macho cursed as her nails dug into his flesh, but he didn't stop her.

"Ooohhh, Antonio…Antonio," she moaned out as she started speeding up, bouncing on his dick like it was her pogo stick. "Antonio!"

"Yes! Scream my name!"

"Antonio!"

SMACK!

"Aye!" he shouted when G-Baby slapped the shit out of him. "What the hell is wrong with you!"

"Antoniooooo!" she yelled, then smacked him again and again and again.

SMACK! SMACK! SMACK!

"Stop hittin' me, Gabi!" Macho yelled.

"Antonio!" she again shouted then she smacked him again.

***

Macho jumped awake and saw Yessy staring down at him, with one eyebrow raised up. She was standing over him, wearing her silk nightgown. Looking around, he realized that he was in bed, in his boxers. Donnell Jones crooned from the speakers mid-volume.

"Hey? Antonio?" he heard Yessy say.

He looked up at her.

"Are you okay?" she asked.

"Did you smack me?"

She started smiling. "Nope. Did you have a good dream, though? You was moaning like you was in a porno."

"Um… I don't remember," he lied.

Yessy looked down at the tent in his boxer briefs. She smiled then reached down to the hem of her nightgown and pulled it up and over her head, revealing her nakedness to him.

"Well…how about I give you something real wet and good to dream about for real," she said, before dropping down to straddle his lap.

"Um…okay," he said while she pulled his Polos off and tossed them away.

Yessy sat her dripping wet pussy on top of his bone-hard dick and started kissing on his neck, trailing her lips down to his chest. Macho laid there tripping his ass off.

What in the actual fuck was that? he asked himself, as Yessy went lower…and lower…and lower.

When he felt her lift up off him, slide down, and let her warm mouth take his dick in, all thoughts of the hot sexy threesome dream dissipated…for now.

Chapter 7

Constant ringing woke Macho up out of his sex-induced slumber. Yessy was naked as she slept peacefully satisfied next to him, with one leg over his, and her head resting on his chest. As the ringing made Macho stir, she groaned in her sleep.

"You should've put it on silent, baby," she said to him.

He reached over to his nightstand to grab the phone. Focusing his eyes on the screen, he saw a name and number that instantly pissed him off.

"On everything I love, Jamal," he said as he answered the call. "If you wakin' me up at …," he paused and looked at the tie on the screen of his phone. "3:37 in the morning on a Saturday for some bullshit, I will blow your house up."

He heard the young Middle Eastern guy start talking, sounding panicked.

"No, bro! I swear, it's not bullshit!" Jamal claimed. "I need your help! For real, Macho! Please, man! I got cars that my uncle is threatening to crush if I don't' get them out of his salvage yard."

"And I give a fuck, why?"

"You know why, bro! I got merch in them! They are fully loaded!" Jamal told him.

"Again…and?"

"My normal guy quit on me last minute, bro!"

"I wonder why. Could it be because you be wakin' muthafuckaz up while they sleep to save yo' dumbass from problems you wouldn't have if you planned ahead?" asked Macho.

"Macho! Please, bro! I will pay you top dollar for your time!"

"How many cars?"

Yessy's eyes popped open when she heard her man sound like he was about to accept a job while they should be resting.

"Seven, bro! Can you help me? Come on, Macho! I need them today! My buyers have been waiting for twenty-four hours already! They're pissed!"

"Today, huh? If I get up outta my warm bed, next to my warm beautiful lady, I need forty grand per car."

"What? Forty thousand?"

"Take it or leave it, pendejo."

"Antonio, just hang up on him. Fuck that shit, bae," Yessy groaned, wanting to go back to sleep.

"Come on, Macho! Lemme' give you twenty gees! Hook me up, man!"

"I will slap the shit out of you if you disrespect me again. Matter of fact, I'm hangin' up right now."

"Noo! Okay! Okay, Macho! Alright! Forty grand! I'll pay you the forty per car!" Jamal quickly agreed. "Just, pleeeaase, go get them right now!"

"Ha! Fuck you think I am? Stupid? Wire the money, now, to that account number that I know you still have," Macho said, knowing that the young dude had a reputation for trying to be a slickster.

"Okay! I'll call you right back!" Jamal told him and hung up.

"Antonio freakin' Valdez…why is it that you constantly allow money to be the reason to keep doing business with shady people? Especially when you are actually already filthy rich," Yessy asked.

Macho shrugged as his iPhone dinged. He saw the notification on the screen notifying him that a two hundred eighty thousand dollar deposit was put into his private account by a code name that he knew was Jamal.

"The answer to your question is because…I love the dough more than you know! Wooooo!" he sang out suddenly.

Yessy stared at him with a blank expression while he stretched, shoulder-bumping her, wiggling his eyebrows and grinning.

"You're an asshole," she told him.

"No, I am not! I am eeell tiguuereeeee," he shouted, then rolled on top of her and started kissing all over her face.

Yessy couldn't help but bust out laughing at him. "Oh my God, yo, you are mad crazy, Antonio."

His phone rang again. He reached for it and answered Jamal's call.

"Twice in less than ten minutes, you interrupting my mode," he said.

"Macho, bro! Come on, man! I sent you the money! How long?" Jamal whined.

"Five hours to get there, about forty-five minutes to get loaded, five hours back. Add in that I have to pre-trip my truck and trailer, which takes about half an hour, then add in the possibility of traffic, speed traps, bathroom breaks and—"

"Macho!" Jamal shouted impatiently.

"See you around four o'clock, pendejo. And as always, thank you for choosing Numero Uno. Goodbye!" Macho told him, then ended the call.

He looked back down at Yessy. She stared up at him with a frown. He smiled at her. She shook her head.

"You're gonna make me kick your ass," she told him.

"I hear you talkin', punk. Come on," he said, rolling off of her and hopping off the bed. "I need my queen with me. The more help I have, the faster it goes, then we can get back and take your machines to the job site."

***

After they showered, Macho and Yessy got dressed. Macho threw on a plain t-shirt, 501 Levi's jeans, and Timberlands. Yessy put on a black shirt with "NUYORICAN QUEEN" in silver letters across her breasts, then slid on a tight black leather mini skirt. Shek put on her blow low top Air Force 1s with silver Nike swooshes and laces, put her hair in a ponytail, then put on some black eyeliner, and glossy black lipstick.

When Macho saw her emerge from their massive walk-in closet, he shook his head, hating how good she looked when he needed to focus.

"Why you gotta wear a skirt when we on business, bae?" he asked her.

She gave him a devious smirk. "You did say how sexy I look in a skirt with a gun in my hand," she reminded him.

Macho chuckled. "Great. I get stuck with a hard dick all day until we get back home," he said sarcastically.

Yessy stepped up to him. "Or…" she said, grabbing at the crotch of his jeans, "…since you are such a good man…I might be willing to help you out a little."

A second later, his pants and boxer briefs were down at his ankles, his woman on her knees before him, and his dick was down her throat. Yessy sucked his cock like a porn-star on cocaine and molly until he exploded in her mouth. She spit his cum out onto his dick, then like a kitten lapping up milk, she slurped it all back up and swallowed it.

"Feel better?" she asked him as he helped her up from her knees.

"Maybe…how about a little—"

"Nope," she said, taking a step back as he tried to reach for the hem of her skirt to pull it up. "Later for all that. You woke me up to go haul ya' punk ass friend's cars so let's go get it done, then maybe you can get some of this cinnamon strudel cookie."

Macho shook his head. "Mean ass porkchop."

"Shut-up, nigga," Yessy shot back, then sauntered off, switching her wide hips extra hard, knowing his eyes were on her phat, juicy leather-clad ass.

***

Yessy went to wake G-Baby up so she could tell her that she and Macho would be back later. G-Baby didn't want to be left, so she hurried out of bed, got showered and dressed, while Macho got the dogs fed.

***

Thirty minutes later, G-Baby came down the stairs from her half of the luxurious home, dressed in a purple shirt that said "CHICAGO" on it in blue letters, blue leggings, and down on her feet she rocked purple Air Max 90s with blue laces and blue swooshes. Her hair, braided into two neat cornrows, was covered in a purple Chicago fitted that had a green Chicago Bear on it.

Macho did all he could to keep his mind focused on the mission, instead of G-Baby and the freaky dream he had about her and his woman. They all hopped into Yessy's G-Wagon and on the way to the yard, Yessy made a pit-stop at McDonald's for breakfast sandwiches and hash browns.

***

Yessinia

Arriving at the entrance to the yard, Yessy came to a stop about eighty feet from the turn-in when she saw Shane, one of the twins that drove for Macho, making a wide right turn, to head in the direction she was coming from. The silver 2006 Peterbilt 379 tri-axle heavy-hauler he was driving was coupled to a very expensive Low-boy trailer. His brother Mane turned out after him, in a black 2005 tri-axle 379

Extended Hood Peterbilt pulling an identical Low-boy. They were both heading to pick up the heavy Caterpillar construction machines that G-Baby had booked for them.

The twins tooted their air horns at their bosses as they turned out, motoring east to get to the highway. Yessy beeped back and turned in.

Down in the yard, Yessy saw the ladies that she and G-Baby had hired, after they all had discharged from the military tucker unit they both had been in charge of, in which Yessy was still in charge of, until her up-and-coming discharge date. The ladies that were there were all loaded with construction machines that Yessy and G-Baby owned for their big construction and demolition business.

Chloe's International 9900i Eagle heavy-hauler, custom painted turquoise and decked out with a lot of chrome and stainless-steel, was sitting off to the side of the lot, lights on and engine idling. Her truck, also hooked to a Low-boy, had one of Yessy and G-Baby's big and heavy Caterpillar excavators chained down on it.

Next to Chloe's Eagle, was Lauren's white Kenworth T600 heavy-hauler with a Low-boy hooked up to it. Chained down on it was Yessy's and G-Baby's front-end wheel loader. Perla, in her Peterbilt 367 heavy-hauler, had Yessy's and G-Baby's biggest excavator, a Caterpillar 345 C, that weighed just under the hundred thousand pounds by itself, chained down on her Low-boy.

"They be on biz', Joe," G-Baby said appreciatively of how their ladies were always on point when it came to business, as she balled up the wrapper to her sausage, egg, and cheese McGriddle.

"Tati, Maria, Dee-Dee, and Tiffany gon' take the D10s and the D8s," Macho added as he looked at the two gigantic Caterpillar D10 bulldozers, that sat as tall as a small house, and the three D8 bulldozers that weren't that much smaller than the D10s.

"Let's hope they all stay motivated for if we make that move happen," Yessy said, hoping that soon, she'd get the call that would put her, G-Baby, and Numero Uno Transport on a whole new level.

***

The three wasted no time in getting El Viejo pre-tripped for the ride. Macho climbed right up into the cab and got out a paper-log book from the glove compartment. On an official capacity, Macho was treating the job as a legit run, so he needed to log the trip accordingly, in case the overzealous state troopers, especially in Michigan, decided to pull him over and check him all the way out.

Since El Viejo was so old, the engine did not have a connection for an Electronic Logging Device to be plugged in, in which now, its E-Logs were recently made mandatory, by the Department of Transportation, for rigs hauling interstate commerce. Certain trucks that were old, or newer, but had older engines without E-Log plugs, were exempt from having E-Logs, but paper-logs still had to be kept. The entire trip, including fueling, getting weighted, loading/unloading, rests/breaks, and maintenance, had to be logged.

Macho grabbed a plastic ruler and pencil from the glove compartment, and he drew a line that came in from the left side of the paper, onto what was designated as Line 3, putting himself onto "On Duty/Not-Driving" duty status, which was the option to select while the mandatory pre-trip inspection was being performed.

***

Yessy unlatched the old Pete's heavy iron engine hood, then she and G-Baby checked the engine bay. All the fluid reservoirs were full, the suspension was in working order, and the wiring inside had no cracks or frays.

G-Baby used a bright light to check under the engine where the oil pan was. She saw no fresh leaks at all. She then shined the light under where the transmission was and saw no leaks there either. Nodding her head, she cut the light off and stool back up, just as Macho was climbing up behind the wheel.

He pushed the clutch pedal in, making sure the shifter was in neutral, then he turned the key and fired the powerful engine up. El Viejo shook as the Cat roared out of the pipes. He got goose bumps like always.

Yessy and G-Baby waved as the Numero Uno ladies started rolling off with the machines to go and drop them off at the job site. With the dashboard lights on, monitoring the gauges as the air pressure, oil pressure, oil temperature, all started rising along with the voltmeter and water/coolant temperature. Macho took his iPhone out to text Evelyn.

"Yo, lil' cuzzin. I need to use one of your car-handler trailers," he texted her.

He looked at the needles in the air pressure gauge rising up as the truck's air compressor-built air, filling up the air tank.

He got a reply back from Evelyn as the air pressure reached 125psi.

"Why?" she asked him, with a confused face emoji.

Macho texted her back. "Got some cars to haul…duh!"

His phone rang seconds later. As he answered Evelyn's call, the passenger's door opened up and Dreams jumped up inside, followed by Maliante. Dreams climbed up onto his lap and started licking his face excitedly, while Maliante ran and jumped onto the bed in the sleeper.

"Who you talking crazy to like that, cabrón?" she asked sassily.

"The truck driving version of Cardi-B," replied Macho with a chuckle as G-Baby climbed up into the truck and went back into the sleeper.

Yessy climbed up and took her seat, up in the cab with her man, ready to hit the road.

Macho heard his baby cousin smack her lips. "Antonio… I will beat cho' ass if you call me her again, dude."

He laughed. "Just like Cardi-B…crazy…and drunk as fuck."

"Whatever, primo. Don't be scrapping my trailer, man."

"Like Nena does?" Macho shot back, chuckling at the memories of Evelyn's wild-ass mix-breed driver chick having wrecked plenty of trucks and trailers in the past.

Evelyn busted out laughing. "No comment!" she said then the call ended.

Chapter 8

As El Viejo idled, Macho used the ruler to draw a line down to Line 4, taking his duty status from "Not Driving," to "Driving."

He tossed the log book back on the dash, tucked the pencil and the ruler with it, then clutched El Viejo's transmission into reverse and backing away from Bay #2, he clutched into first and headed to exit the yard.

***

GZA's "Breaker, Breaker" pounded from the woofers as Macho headed north on Green Bay Road. He re-entered Zion, but keeping on Green Bay, the state line road between Illinois and Wisconsin.

He got to Russell Road and hit a left before the yellow light at the intersection turned red. Heading west on Russell, he nodded his head to the beat, mouthing the words to the second verse.

Yessy had her iPhone out, playing "Angry Birds," entertaining herself by launching angry birds at the annoying green pigs.

Laid out on the bed, G-Baby played with Maliante's ears, flipping and flopping them, making him try to nip at her fingers. She laughed and kept on teasing him until he farted, which made her have to slide the rear sleeper window open and fan his funk away.

Approaching Russell and Kilbourne Road, Macho saw a customized heavy-haul semi with amber-colored strobe lights flashing brightly and an Oversize Load banner on the front bumper, making a wide left turn out onto Russell, pulling a Low-boy with an asphalt-scraping machine on it. Macho slowed down for the flashy rig to have enough room.

He reached for the Cobra CB radio, turned it on. Still on Channel 19, the national trucker channel, he grabbed the mike off the hook and spoke into it.

"Aye there, driver, that looks like a big-money load there, come one," he said in a country trucker twang.

Seconds after the rig's turn was complete, he heard his cousin Xavier reply back.

"Naw. Doin' a favor for Big Oso, cuz," Xavier told him, as his big Cummins engine roared out of the two giant exhaust stacks while he rolled towards Green Bay Road. "Everything aight?" he then asked as Macho came to the intersection with his right turn signal on.

"For now," Macho replied, making the turn onto Kilbourne.

"Sounds like you haven't heard," Xavier said as Macho slow rolled towards where the Valdez Transports yard was.

"Heard what?" Macho said.

A second later, his phone rang. He answered Xavier's call right away.

"A lot of people been getting' scooped up off the streets, cuz. Overdosin' on that hot shit, yah mean?"

"Okay…You sayin' that like it's my fault or something, nigga," Macho replied as he came upon the entrance to PJ&D Transport LLC, a massive trucking company started by Macho's deceased great uncle Pedro, along with his grandfather Juanito, and his second great uncle Diego. The Kilbourne yard was ChaCha's personal dispatch spot.

"Well…it's our shit that's makin' it happen, cuz," Xavier told him.

“Our shit? Man, cut it the fuck out, yo. Ain’t nothin’ in it to make anybody drop and get to foamin’ out they mouths.”

“That’s what I said,” Xavier replied, right as Macho approached the entrance to Javi’s truck yard, “but when I heard this, I made some calls. Someone’s been coppin’, but addin’ they own lil’ thang to it, and it's bad, cuz. Real bad.”

Macho glanced over and saw Yessy wearing the same shocked expression that he had on.

“Who else has heard about this, since I haven’t, until now?” he asked Xavier, coming to a complete stop.

“Javi heard, and ChaCha, not sure if Danny has, but yo, cuz…we gon’ have to get on top of this. You know who gon’ be tryna come holla if the finger gets to pointin’ at us ‘n shit.”

“Aight, One, cuz,” Macho said.

“Yup. Love, nigga.”

“What in the hell? Someone’s cuttin the coke with poison?” Yessy said, looking at him with wide eyes.

“Somebody wants to die,” Macho said, shaking his head. “Fuck would anyone do some dumbass shit to the most supreme cocaine in the United States of fucking America for?”

***

Inside one-acre yard of Valdez Transport, LLC, Macho saw six trucks heading to the exit. He saw Evelyn in her big burnt-orange Volvo 880, pulling one of her fifty-three-foot long, luxury enclosed six-car Kentucky car-carrier trailers, that was painted to match her truck. It was very similar to a NASCAR transport trailer.

Behind her was her girlfriend Gloria, in her glossy black and chrome Kenworth T660, pulling an identical luxury enclosed car-carrier that was also painted to match the truck.

Nena was in a newer red Peterbilt 389, pulling another luxury-enclosed car-carrier, and behind her were three of the guys that were in Javi’s intermodal/dry-van/refrigerated freight crew, all coupled to fifty-three-foot long dry-van trailers. The three men all shouted out to Macho over the CB. He replied back, telling them all to have safe trips.

"I can't stand lookin' at that creepy-ass truck, cuz," Macho heard Evelyn say through the radio.

"Close ya' eyes then," he said to her, pointing El Viejo in the direction of where Evelyn's spare car-transport trailers were parked.

"Don't listen to her, Macho," he heard Gloria say. "I think ol' school is the way to roll. No computers, all muscle."

"Yeah," he then heard Nena agree.

"Both of you dick-ridin' bitches, shut the fuck up and mind your business," Evelyn shot back at them.

"Bitch, suck a dick, pendeja!" Gloria fired back, then the three turned out of the yard, leaving Macho, Yessy, and G-Baby laughing their asses off.

***

He rolled towards Evelyn's car-transport crew's parking area, where along with four steel exposed rack seven-car trailers and two 8-car carriers sat, there were six Peterbilt 389s. They were built to be able to transport ten vehicles at once.

As quickly as he could, Macho got El Viejo backed up to a seven-car transporter trailer, then got hooked up and checked out both his ol' school Pete and the trailer. In just under forty minutes, he was ready to roll out.

Macho hopped back up into the Pete and pulled off, exiting Javi's yard as a few vehicles belonging to more of his drivers arrived for work. He honked at the big dual diesel Ford pick-up truck that belonged to the massive Samoan that everyone called Tank, which was followed by a newer GMC Yukon XL Denali, driven by O-Boy, and behind O-Boy was Bull, driving a Mercedes GL550.

Macho made a wide turn out onto Kilbourne and headed back towards Russell, to take it down to the interstate. As he approached the intersection, he saw Javi's silver 1967 Pontiac GTO convertible turn onto Kilbourne from off Russell. He saw his younger cousin behind the wheel. Next to Javi was his wife and one of their big Cane Corsos in front of her, head hanging out the side to let the wind blow in her face. In the rear was their two children, Javi Jr. and Amara, with the second Cane Corso sitting next to them, being the protective alpha male that he was.

Macho tapped the touch screen, brought up Javi's number and called him.

"What up, cuzzo?" the green-eyed goon answered.

"What's this I'm hearin' about someone playin' wit' the merch?" he asked as he came to a stop at the light at Russell.

"Maaaaaan, I have no clue, but nigga, that shit got me hot. I told Eve to have' Lil' Five and his Lord homies to find out who' dumpin' it. It's on when they do, cuz."

"Bet," Javi replied.

Yessinia

Yessy brooked hard as The Lox's "Ryde Or Die Bitch" bumped. She was perturbed about hearing that someone was cutting her man's family's cocaine, with something that was killing people. That was very bad business. She wasn't even a dope girl, but it had her ready to go kick in some doors and find out what the coke was being cut with, and who was doing it.

Thinking hard himself, Macho blazed a trail down the hammer lane, heading south towards Chicago. The sky had turned light blue as daybreak came. Barely any traffic was out. People were still either just getting up or still sleeping off a wild weekend.

Looking back into the sleeper, Yessy saw that G-Baby was still sleeping on her stomach. Maliante laid next to her, his chin resting on her bubble booty. Yessy snickered to herself, then turned back and looked over at her man, as he shifted into 17th-high.

Turning down the music, Yessy said to Macho, "I know there are things we need to concentrate on when we get back, but I can't wait to see if we get this military contract, bae," speaking up so Macho could hear her over the loud roar of El Viejo's engine. "It's really gonna take us to a whole new ball game."

He nodded in agreement. "I was floored when you told me about it. I never thought about somethin' like that comin' to our company before."

Yessy gasped. "You said our company!"

He smiled, glancing over at her. "Yes. That's what it is, baby. Ours. You already knew that, though."

"I mean…I…" She had no clue what to say at that.

Macho chuckled. "It's all good, amor. Don't trip about the future, though, either. You and Gabi deserve everything y'all put ya minds to. I have never met more stronger minded women in my life than you two. Best believe, y'all gon get it. And it'll all be thanks to you and the Gangsta Boo for makin' Numero Uno Transport's reputation grow. You two are the epitome of dope. Yessy, On my dead Homiez, yo."

His words meant so much to her. She hadn't grown up with much in her life, except for her brother. She didn't have family, and she didn't really have friends, besides for her man's family and G-Baby. Being taken in by such good people and being held in the strong arms of the man she loved with all of her heart, every night, was something Yessy never thought would be for her to have.

Nodding her head with a smile, Yessy leaned back in the seat and closed her eyes. In just minutes, with Dreams next to her, she drifted off to a peaceful sleep.

***

Macho flew through Chicago breezing along briskly. After he rolled through the I-Pass lane at the Chicago Skyway Toll booth, he crossed over a narrow bridge and soon entered Gary, Indiana. As he rolled, he started thinking about a major renovation project in New York that he had going on, right across from Central Park. Glancing over at Yessy, then quickly glancing back at the sleeping G-Baby, Macho smiled, dying for the day where he got to show them what he had for them to get there. He knew they were gonna go bananas.

Macho

He crossed into Gary, Indiana, and headed east. Staying on I-94, as the East West Toll Road split away from it, he got to Michigan City, Indiana and still on I-94, followed the highway north as it took him into Michigan, through New Buffalo. He passed a northbound weigh station, but since it was closed, he kept on rolling north, running along Lake Michigan. When Macho got to Benton Harbor, I-94 curved and started back east. He kept turning and burning, passing Portage, and Kalamazoo. After he passed Battle Creek, he felt his stomach begin to rumble with hunger, and glancing down at the dashboard, he saw El Viejo needed diesel.

Seeing exit signs for Lansing. Macho switched lanes, getting over into the granny-lane to get off. When the exit came into view, he reached out to the dashboard and hit the switch, turning the jake brake on. The loud roar woke Yessy and G-Baby up. Macho worked the brakes to slow the rig, which contrary to what most would think, was a little harder to do since no trailer was coupled. A semi with no trailer was harder to stop, since there was no weight on the rear wheels. Having the weight there is what helped the brakes of a big truck work the best. Macho down-shifted the 18-speed transmission, breaking it down like a pro, the truck roared louder every time he took it down a gear. The smile that grew on his face was that of whenever he broke it down while he drove. He loved the sound of a powerful Caterpillar engine as much as a true gangster loved rapid-fire blasts of an AK-47.

Yessy yawned as he exited the interstate. Ice Cube's "Hello," featuring Dr Dre and MC Ren, bumped.

"Y'all hungry?" Macho asked, coming to a stop at a red light.

"Hell yeah!" G-Baby answered first.

"Definitely," Yessy added, as Dreams got up and laid her big meaty head on Yessy's thigh, "and so is my baby! Yes, you are, you fat-head killer you!" she cooed, making Dreams reach up and lick her face.

The light turned green, Macho rolled off and made his way to where a Pilot truck stop was. He entered the medium size rest stop and headed around the designated truck route, coming to the fuel-up station first. A few other rigs were getting filled up when he pulled up to a pump. He put the shifter in neutral and applied the tractor's brakes, then shutting off the engine, he grabbed the logbook, pencil and ruler, then drew a line up from Line 3, to Line 1, taking himself to "Off Duty."

Macho set the logbook back up on the dash and was about to open his door, when he noticed the truck, a dark-blue Volvo 730 displaying PJ&D Transport, LLC on the passenger's door, with Cicero, Illinois under it, along with the D.O.T. numbers, and the MC numbers. It was coupled to a flatbed trailer, loaded with two big rolls of steel. He smiled to himself, loving that he damn near saw his family's trucks everywhere he went since PJ&D had just over 4,000 semis running all fifty states.

Then, his smile faded when he saw the driver of the rig climb from behind the Volvo's big sleeper, with the diesel fuel pump in her hand, carrying it to fuel up the passenger's side tank.

"What's wrong, bae?" Yessy asked, noticing how he froze.

He looked at her. "Um…"

Macho nodded his head at who he saw, then, rolling his eyes to the right, where G-Baby was in the sleeper, held a finger up to his lips to tell his woman not to say anything.

With furrowed brows, Yessy got up and looked out his window.

"Oh shit…" she said quietly, looking at her man with the same worried look in his eyes.

Chapter 9

G-Baby

"What is y'all looking at?" asked G-Baby, as she and Maliante moved towards the cab area.

"Nothing!" Yessy said, way too panicky for G-Baby to not realize she was capping.

G-Baby twisted her lips up as Yessy did her best to not make eye contact.

"Gabi, don't flip out, okay?" Macho said then, glancing up at her over his right shoulder.

"Flip out over what, Joe? Y'all asses need to stop actin' weird?"

"Your sister's outside," Yessy told her. "Fueling her truck up."

G-Baby didn't say anything. She remained quiet for a minute, but inside, hearing that her sister was there, made her feel like her blood was boiling.

Macho and Yessy knew how much G-Baby despised her youngest sister. Their beef stemmed from so long ago, but due to the nature of its beginning, it was still so hard for G-Baby to not want to strangle her sister.

"Gabi?" Yessy said. "Can you be cool while we're here? We're just passing through, like she is."

G-Baby put on a fake smile. "Sure," she said. "Can we get out? I'm hungry."

***

Yessinia

Getting out of El Viejo, Yessy ushered G-Baby towards the building. They both couldn't help but look at where the slightly smaller version of G-Baby stood, fueling her truck up.

The younger Gangsta Boo was the spitting image of her big sister. She was five-five, twenty-three years old, and was just as voluptuous as big sis. Her skin was the color of caramel, just like Yessy's skin, and she had long dark hair. She was dressed in a PJ&D Transport work shirt, with tight fitting denim jeans that had cuts on the front of the legs. On her feet, she rocked a pair of Timberlands, and her hair was pulled back into a neat ponytail.

She saw Yessy first, then her sister. They both saw her smirking at them with taunting eyes.

G-baby attempted to shake Yessy and go get the girl. Yessy grabbed her shirt and pulled her back. They didn't need to spill blood on diesel-soaked concrete.

Macho

Outside of his old Pete, Macho did everything he could to ignore G-Baby's little sister, but when she saw him, she refused to let him be.

"Hiiiii, Macho," she sang out to him.

Ignoring her, he grabbed the fuel pump and uncapped the driver's side tank, inserting the nozzle in to start filling.

"I know you hear me," she said to him.

He kept on ignoring her, his back turned to her, looking up at the open driver's window, where Maliante's head stuck out. He could see the Rottweiler was looking at G-Baby's sister. He started growling seconds later.

Right when Maliante started barking angrily, which caused Dream to start barking, Macho felt a tap on his shoulder.

"Excuuuuse me, sir?" he heard behind him.

Groaning, Macho told Maliante to be quiet, then he turned to see the mini G-Baby there, smiling up at him.

"What do you want, Mariela?" he asked her.

"I wanted to say hi. I haven't seen you in a while. How you been?" she asked, with a sneaky smile on her face.

"I been great," he told her, not even attempting to ask how she had been.

"Good. I've been well. I see you still got my sister hanging around you and your lady. How's that working for you?"

"G-Baby is our best friend. How you think things been workin' out, shortie?"

"Well…she's always around you and hasn't had a man in…how many years?"

Macho shook his head at her. "You should probably get back to your truck. Someone likely needs that pump."

Mariela giggled. "They can wait. I'm having a conversation with one of the most desirable men in the Midwest."

"Mari…my dogs are angry that you're here," he said as the two continued grunting and growling. "They can jump through the window…just sayin."

Mariela looked up and her eyes met Maliante's. He started growling even more viciously, baring his teeth at her.

"Awww! He's so cuuuute! I wanted a Rottweiler, but they're expensive, and I don't have patience to train a pup. Maybe you could help me?" she asked, batting her eyes at him.

"No."

"Aw, come on, Macho. Don't be mean to me. I'm your best friend's baby sister."

"No…what are you going to be, is beat up, if you don't leave. Gabi is still ready to pound cho' face in for that shit you pulled when y'all lived together. Bounce before I tell Yessy to let her."

Macho knew of the crazy relationship between G-Baby and her little sister. Growing up in Humboldt Park, the two hung out with two different Latin Folks mobs, which had beef with each other. G-Baby hung with a set of Maniac Latin Disciples, while Mariela hung with some Insane Spanish Cobras. The rivalry between the two gangs had found its way into the Medina household, and since G-Baby was older, and was held to a higher expectation from their mother and father, she was the one that got kicked out and ended up being sent to live with her grandmother up in Wauk-Town.

"Macho, Macho, Macho…you might not realize this, but my sister and I are alike. She is fearless, and so am I. But, I'll go. Just know, I will see y'all around."

At that, she turned and sauntered off, swaying her wide hips hard as she figured his eyes were on her.

Macho shook his head as he watched her walk away. Turning back to El Viejo, he looked up and saw Maliante, still looking at Mariela.

"Tranquilo, boy. She's gone," he told the black and rust-colored beast.

Maliante licked his chops…but his eyes still stayed locked onto her.

Yessinia

From the Chester's Chicken restaurant inside the Pilot, Yessy ordered four chicken sandwiches, for her and her man, along with potato wedges and grape soda. G-Baby got herself chicken tenders, fries and Mountain Dew. While they waited, Yessy saw G-Baby looking through the convenience store window, which gave a view of the truck fueling section. They could see Marela pulling off from the pump. Macho was still filling up the driver's side tank.

"Why the hell would ChaCha hire my bitch ass sister, man? The door said Cicero, it's not from the Kilbourne yard."

G-Baby turned and looked at Yessy. "Yessinia…ChaCha runs all of PJ&D!"

"Shhh!" Yessy reached out a hand and playfully mushed G-Baby in her face.

G-Baby retaliated by booty-bumping Yessy, hard enough to nearly make her fall.

"Ha! What, biatch!" G-Baby teased.

Other people in line and waiting for their orders laughed at the two Boricuas. Yessy nodded her head and told her bestie that she would have her revenge.

G-Baby looked out the window at where Macho was just finishing up. She sighed to herself.

"Whatcha' lookin' at?" Yessy asked, putting an arm around G-Baby's neck.

"Uh…El Viejo," G-Baby capped.

"You look like you wanna fuck him."

G-Baby scoffed. "Fuck a truck?"

Yessy let her go and looked down into her eyes. "Is that what you wanna fuck?"

"What the hell does that mean?" asked G-Baby, with furrowed eyebrows.

Yessy started laughing. "Nothing at all, sissy boo. I know you wouldn't look at Antonio like that. You saw what happened to the last bitch that looked at him with wet-pussy eyes."

G-Baby did indeed remember, and it gave her chills up her spine. Yessy was a true monster when it came to her man.

"Why are you saying this?" she asked Yessy, just as the order server called them for their food.

"I'm just messin' wit you, Gabi, damn! Relax, punk-ass!" Yessy said to her.

But G-Baby didn't believe it. She swallowed hard at the thought of Yessy somehow starting to realize that she had feelings for Macho. It would be the worst possible thing to happen if the Nuyorican figured it out.

***

Picking a table by a window that looked out towards the non-commercial vehicle parking area and the street, Yessy and G-Baby sat down and waited for Macho to come in. He entered minutes later, after he'd gone and parked El Viejo. As he approached the table, Yessy saw he was talking on the phone using his Bluetooth earpiece.

He sat next to her, kissed her cheek, and continued talking.

"Tell her I said what up, and we'll be back a little later, bro."

Yessy figured he was talkin to Tool.

"Nigga, I said I got chu'. Chill out. As long as the money is on deck, then I'm on it for you, bro," Macho said, then took his phone out of his pocket and ended the call.

Todo bien, papi?" asked Yessy.

"Yep!" he replied excitedly, rubbing his hands together. "Just a business call," he capped.

"New business?" G-Baby asked.

"Well don't keep us in suspense, Antonio. What is it?" asked Yessy, turning to face him.

Instead of telling her what he had really been on the phone about, he brought up the new business venture that he and his brother had been planning for a while, and were finally ready to start making it happen.

Yessy and G-Baby were geeked.

"Oh my God! Bae, that shit sounds dope as hell, yo!" Yessy exclaimed.

"On the real, Joe! That's genius!" G-Baby added. "Starting your own truck and trailer dealership and adding custom chrome shop to bring a lot of customers!"

Macho's plans to build dealerships and sell, and/or lease commercial trucks and trailers, had been put together with his brother's glider-kit truck building business. New and used trucks and trailers could be sold or leased as is, or customers that had some money could have their purchases taken right next to where the main service and display garages would be, and have their rides decked out so when they pulled out, they pulled off like bosses.

"And I need y'all to help to build every location up," Macho added. "You two have carte blanche to do what y'all do on every building."

"Got it," Yessy said, excited and ready to dive in.

"We gotta find at least three locations first," he then said, "I need at least an acre per property, and I'd prefer one in Illinois, one in Wisconsin and one around Pittsburgh."

"I wish Kenzie was still around," G-Baby said, speaking of Xavier's ex, that had mysteriously vanished two years ago with her daughter, breaking Xavier's heart in two from how in love with the red head beauty and her precious daughter he'd been. "Kenzie was good at finding great deals on bare residential and commercial land."

Yessy nodded her head, agreeing. "I still can't believe she just up and left. Yo, I think Xavier is still hurting over that, even if he is with Vanessa."

"I know who isn't broke up about it," Macho said, after chewing a mouthful of chicken sandwich.

The girls looked at him.

"Who? Everyone loved Kenzie, bae," Yessy said.

He looked at her. "Nena."

"Oh." Yessy shook her head. "She doesn't count. Nena hates every female Xavier's dick ever went into."

Macho busted out laughing. "Okay. Let's finish eating. I'm tryna get these cars and get back to the ILL-state so dude can get the fuck up off my nuts."

Chapter 10

After Macho fed Dreams and Maliante a bunch of unseasoned chicken patties and gave them water, he and Yessy took them for a short walk, while G-Baby gave El Viejo a quick check over. When the dogs did their business, Yessy and Macho headed back to the truck, ready to go.

"Let Gabi drive the rest of the way, bae." Yessy noticed that her man looked tired.

He nodded, just as a yawn escaped him. "Wanna drive, Gangsta Boo?" he asked, right as she shut El Viejo's engine hood.

"You bet cho' ass I do!" she replied, excited as hell to drive the powerful ol' school Peterbilt again.

***

Kicking off his Timbs, Macho laid back on the bed. G-Baby started El Viejo's engine and grabbed the logbook, drawing a line back down to Line 4, putting herself onto 'On Duty' status.

G-Baby actually had her Class A CDL, with all the endorsements, compared to Yessy still only have a military commercial vehicle certification. Since discharging, G-Baby had gotten her CDL through the Illinois Secretary of State's Military "Even Exchange" licensing program. It allowed her and other former military personnel that had been discharged, with a job opening driving a commercial vehicle immediately after leaving the service, to bypass taking any of the CDL knowledge and skills tests. Being employed by Numero Uno Transport helped her get her L's and from time to time, she went on trips with Macho, sharing behind the wheel time as he delivered high-dollar freight all over the Midwest, and East Coast. It wasn't easy being alone with him, but she managed to keep it professional…until now.

***

Making the dogs stay up in the cab with G-Baby, Yessy closed the privacy curtains that separated the cab from the sleeper, then went to join her man on the bed. She kicked off her Air Forces. His phone started ringing just as her butt touched the bed. As he took it out of his pocket, Yessy snatched it away from him.

"Um…why?" he asked, as she powered it off.

"Because," she told him, with a smile loaded with mischief. "My pussy has been calling your name since your dick was down my throat earlier."

"Ooooweeeeee!" he said as they heard and felt G-Baby pulling off from where he had parked El Viejo. "You ain't said shit but a word! Damelaaaa!"

Macho grabbed her and put her on her back and started kissing her wildly. Yessy's temperature shot sky high as their tongues danced while their lips boxed. His hands caressed her sides, just as Philly's Most Wanted's "Cross The Border," started playing.

His hands slid down to her hips, then her thighs. They came to the hem of her little skirt and started pushing it up, exposing that she didn't have on any panties. He looked up at her and saw the sexiest smile on her face.

"You had this planned all along, huh?" he asked her.

"Deja de hablar y mama esta chocha," she told him, opening her legs up for him to dive in.

He obeyed her demand and did his Michael Phelps into her abyss. He kissed her inner thighs and licked them. Yessy's toes curled and she squealed as she felt his lips get closer, and closer to her throbbing center. A second later, she felt him opening her up.

"Mmmmm…ooooo, baby," she moaned, once his lips began French kissing her clit. "Dios Miiiio! That feels so good!"

He pleased her, dining on her like there was nothing tastier than her. He sucked her clit, swirled his tongue around it, and drank her like champagne as she continuously leaked. Minutes after he started, Yessy's legs began to shake. Her body trembled as she approached her climax. With a thought in his head that always got her, Macho started motor-boating her pussy lips, sending a strong vibration shooting through her core that made her scream out from the suddenness of his move.

"Shit!" She shouted after she exploded in his face, "Goddamn you! Fucking motor-mouth!"

Macho busted out laughing as he wiped his wet face. "Don't hate, appreciate the way I eat this pussy up."

"I do," Yessy told him. "Trust me, I do."

"Okay, then shut up and let me handle my business," he told her, and got up off her.

He stripped out of his shirt and dropped his pants. Yessy sat up and eyed his muscular physique. She bit her lip as she grew even more aroused than she was. She loved the Steel City Mafia tattoo that was right above his picture-perfect image of his flashy Legacy Class Peterbilt, which had his mother and father's name etched into the grille, on his right pectoral. A tattoo of her name on his left pec, with a blue rose under it, was her favorite. All the rest of the ink, Taino tribals, money, guns, trucks, added to his thuggishly handsome ruggedness that kept her pussy soaking wet.

"God, you are so handsome," she said, looking up into his eyes.

"What about me?" he asked jokingly, as he dropped his boxer briefs, his bone hard dick pointing right at what he was craving.

Yessy laughed. "Shut up and come fuck me."

He pounced on her. He relieved her of her shirt, then her bra. His name was tatted above her right breast, with his well-known moniker "EL TIGUERE" under it. He made her keep on her skirt, pushed up around her hips, and slid into her wetness, filling her up with all of him.

Yessy cried out in bliss as he went savage on her, beating it up like he was mad at it. He power-fucked her fast and hard, pushing her legs up so that her knees nearly touched her breasts. He went all the way in, hitting the bottom of the pussy. She screamed out his name crying from such intense pleasure. She was seeing stars as he sent her on a trip to oblivion.

G-Baby

Up front with the dogs, cruising at sixty-five miles an hour on I-69 with a steady northbound flow of semi-trucks, G-Baby sighed to herself as she headed to Flint. She knew what was going on just feet behind her. Every so often, she could hear Yessy cry out his name. The way she was screaming and moaning, G-Baby's pussy was getting wet, knowing that Macho was back there putting his pound game to work on his woman. G-Baby's clit throbbed. She was yearning for some love like that to the point that she could taste the sex.

It had been so long since she'd been sexed down by a good man. The more she thought about it, the more Macho's face filled her mind. She wanted him…bad…and it made her feel like a true piece of shit, pining over her best friend.

She knew she was a baaaaaaad ass chick, and she had the type of body that so many other women shelled out thousands of dollars to plastic surgeons to get. She just couldn't find a man that was even half as intriguing as Antonio Tomas Valdez.

It made her feel so horrible about longing for him. Their three-way friendship was the best, sacred and truly meaningful. Yessy and Macho were her family. Hell, she was a millionaire because of them.

G-Baby wished to God that she could just turn off her feelings for him, to stop being so attracted to him. But, being real with herself…she just couldn't. He was everything she wanted in a man. He was awesomely handsome, a straight up boss and a gangster, filthy rich, and most of all, he was the most selfless man she had ever met.

Leaning back in her seat while she kept one hand on the steering wheel, G-Baby felt eyes on her. She glanced over to the right and saw Dreams looking at her, while Maliante's head was poking out the window, enjoying the wind that was blowing in his face.

"Dreams, if you keep staring at me like a weird-ass Boston Terrier, I'ma beat your ass."

Dreams barked at her.

"Shut up!"

Yessinia

"Ssssss…oooooooo…fuuuuuuuck! Antonio! Oh, my God, you fucking freeeeaaaaaak!" Yessy moaned, as she felt his tongue in her ass, swirling around in her booty hole.

On all fours, face down and ass up, she enjoyed the mind-blowing oral pleasure her man was giving to her juicy derriere. He loved eating her ass, and she loved getting her ass ate.

Less than a minute later, she climaxed again, squirting his chin with her juices. Macho licked her clean, then raised himself up. He smacked her ass cheek hard.

"Dime que quieres que te meta este bicho en ese culo jugoso," Macho demanded of her, before he smacked the other cheek.

"Ay!" she shrieked from the sting. "Metemelo en mi culo!"

He smacked her ass again. "Shout that shit!"

"Baaaee!" she whined "Gabi's gonna hear me!"

He smacked her ass again. "¡No me importa un carajo! Dime, ahora mismo!"

"Metemela en mi culooooo!" Yessy screamed out, obeying his command. "Put it in my ass, papi!" she then repeated in English.

Macho spread her meaty butt cheeks apart, spit on her asshole, then he gripped his throbbing cock and put the tip to her chute. He rubbed the tip in his saliva, then started inching his way inside. Yessy hissed as he stretched her out, grabbing and clenching the bed sheet in her hands. She gritted her teeth and prepared to let him give it to her.

"Fuuuuck!" Macho cursed from how tight and warm her anal tract was.

"Ooooo, baby, yeaaaaah! Fuck me! God yes, I love it!" she told him, looking back at him behind her, biting her lip and giving him her sexiest fuck-face.

Macho locked eyes with her and he went in and out. He shouted, "I love you," to her.

She shouted it back, over and over again, until she came again. Minutes after her, Macho felt his nut coming. He pulled his dick out and got onto his feet. Yessy hurried off the bed, fell to her knees and took his cock into her mouth. With one hand, she jerked his dick while she sucked him. When he came, he roared like a bear, filling her mouth up with so much cum that it dribbled out. Yessy swallowed it all with a simile and looked up at him, with a hand still wrapped around his dick.

"You are bad," she told him.

Macho reached down and took her by the hand, pulling her up from her knees.

"So? You got a problem with it?" he asked, staring down into her beautiful brown eyes.

"Not in any way shape or form, papi," she told him, and rose up on her tippy toes to plant one on his lips. "The way you put it on me makes me feel like I can fly."

"Hmmm…that's because I love you. When a man truly loves his woman, pleasing her is as easy as making pancakes."

Yessy laughed. "Some people don't know how to make them. They be burning them n' shit, like Romeo," she told him, for example.

Macho laughed. "That is some funny shit. "Now I am sure G-Baby heard us, so we are once again gonna have to do something nice for her. It's been a while since someone knocked the dust off her egg, and we fuck every three hours, damn near right next to her."

"She's a big girl, Antonio. She doesn't even want a man, at least that's what she told me," Yessy said, "but I guess we could try to fix her up with someone. He just can't be no clown. My sis deserves the best man possible."

Macho felt quick stab of jealousy at the thought of G-Baby being touched by another guy. Yessy saw his eyes go blank. Her eyebrow rose up.

"Hey? What's wrong?" she asked him, cupping his face with her hands.

"Nothing. I just think…we should make sure that whoever we introduce her to, will put her first and treat her like the queen she is. Gabi is a rare gem that nobody will ever find another of, Yessy."

"Aww! Bae, that is so sweet!" She grabbed the tails of his cornrows and pulled him down for a kiss. "Maybe Michelle can help, or maybe even ChaCha. They both know stand-up type guys that can be a good match."

Macho grunted. "Yeah…maybe," he said, completely unenthused about the idea.

Chapter 11

G-Baby

Feeling G-Baby exit the highway, Macho opened the sleeper curtain and got into the passenger's seat. He directed her to the scrapyard, having her navigate El Viejo through the dilapidated neighborhoods until she arrived at the ghetto industrial area of where their destination was.

At a light, Macho told her to make a left. G-Baby did and saw it was a dead-end street, with a big circular turn-around at the other end. She slowly made her way up the small street, coming up on a tall white privacy fence.

"Drop me off at the entrance and go turn around," Macho told her, as G-Baby came to a stop in front of the open entrance to the scrapyard.

He opened the door and hopped out. G-Baby watched him head towards the entrance. Yessy climbed into the passenger's seat.

"What are you waitin' for, biatch? Get us turned around so we can get loaded and go," Yessy said.

G-Baby rolled off and got seventy-eight-feet of tractor-trailer turned around in one swift try. She pulled up and parked just beyond the yard's entrance. She put the brakes on, shifted in neutral. She grabbed the logbook and drew a line up to Line 2, putting herself into "Working/Not Driving" duty status.

Yessy patted her Rottweiler's head, then with gloves on, she got out. G-Baby grabbed work gloves as well and got out of the truck, going right towards the front driver's side of the trailer, where a "pony-motor," a small gas-powered engine that was like a lawn mower engine, was mounted down on a steel plate. It supplied power to the trailer's hydraulics, so that the ramps that held the vehicles could work. She started it up, then as Yessy headed towards the entrance to the scrap yard, G-Baby made her way around the trailer and pulled out the small steel pins that were in the hydraulic beams that raised and lowered the ramps. They were important, because when the top deck was loaded with cars, the pins kept the beams in place so that during transport, the top ramp wouldn't come down and damage the roofs of the vehicles in the trailer's belly.

Inside the vast dirt yard, stacks of smashed vehicles lined the left of the property and to the rear was a mobile trailer office. Two dirty and greasy front-end wheel loaders with long steel forks carried around vehicles that were going to a big car crusher. To the left, Yessy saw a line of cars, with no license plates on them.

Up towards the center of the yard, she saw her man talking to an older man of Arabic descent. He was a little shorter than Macho, with gray hair and a thick beard. He wore a flannel shirt, jeans, and steel-toe boots. Yessy made her way towards them when Macho saw her and waved her over.

"He must be dealt with, Antonio. I know I can trust you to handle this for me," the older man said, with a Middle Eastern accent. "What you find when he is gone, I give you permission to keep and do with as you please."

Yessy saw Macho smirk, nodding his head. He turned to her and gestured for her to come to him. She did. He took her hand and introduced her to the man.

"Bae, this is Mr. Hasan. Mr. Hasan, this is Yessinia, the love of my life," he said.

Mr. Hasan gave her a warm smile and a nod. "Very nice to meet you, young lady. I thank you for assisting him in helping get these cars off of my lot. May Allah keep you all safe while you take them to that piece of crap, nephew of mine."

Yessy nodded her head, then Mr. Hasan took his leave, heading towards his office.

"Keys are in the cars, baby. Let's get em' and get gone," Macho told her.

Macho got into a black 2004 Mercedes S55 AMG. Yessy got in a silver 2012 Cadillac CTS-V. G-Baby entered the yard and got inside an orange 2003 Mitsubishi Eclipse. They rolled the first three out of the yard, lining up with the rear of the trailer which G-Baby had worked the hydraulics and made the top ramp lower down at the rear, with drive-on ramps extended out for the cars to drive up onto the trailer. Macho eased onto the ramp and drove the Benz all the way up, stopping a few inches just before the front wheels reached the steel stop at the tip.

Yessy pulled up behind him, then G-Baby behind her. They all put the emergency brakes on after putting them in park. They cut the engines and took the keys out of the ignitions.

Heading back for three more. Macho hopped into a blue 2004 Ford Focus SVT, Yessy got in a bronze 1997 Pontiac Grand Am, and G-Baby got into the 2010 Ford Mustang GT. Macho put the Focus on the top ramp. Only four could go up top. Once it was parked, he got out and Yessy worked the levers at the side of the trailer, right where the pony-motor was, and raised the top ramp up.

Macho quickly got all four cars chained down, then the Grand AM and Mustang were driven into the belly. While Yessy and G-Baby got the two chained down, Macho went and got the last vehicle, which was a 2006 Chevy Malibu. He put it in the belly's rear, put the e-brake on, got out and took the car keys with him. He got the Malibu chained down, then Yessy worked the lever to pull in the drive-on ramps, while G-Baby went around the trailer to put the pins back in the beams. When they were all in, Yessy lowered the top rack back down into place and cut the pony-motor off.

Just to be safe, Macho went to a small exterior tool compartment door in the driver's side of El Viejo's sleeper and got out a height stick. He went to the Benz since it was the biggest vehicle on top of the trailer and measured the height. He saw he was well under twelve feet and nodded. Most overpasses, tunnels and other low clearances were thirteen feet or more, but as he had first started learning how to drive a truck, he knew not to trust the clearance signs. Roads being repaved over the years, increased or decreased what the actual height of the road really was, so having sufficient space to pass under with a tall load was key.

"Let's ride, beautiful ladies," Macho said, as he put the height stick back up.

G-Baby stifled a smile, hearing him call her beautiful. She felt her nipples get hard at the thought of him being attracted to her, then they went soft, when she told herself that there was no way in hell that Macho had ever looked at her in that type of way before.

Before they hit the road, the dogs were let out to use the bathroom and stretch. Yessy and G-Baby ran up the street with them, then back down, allowing them to burn off a little energy before the five-hour trip back to Illinois. When they got back to El Viejo, Macho told his lady to take the wheel.

"Don't mind if I do, Captain Sexy," she told him, and kissed him before she climbed up behind the wheel.

Pulling off with the heavy load of cars, Yessy maneuvered El Viejo through Flint like a pro, as she always did. Sitting up in the cab with her, Macho was beyond infatuated by how good his women looked driving his truck. It was the ultimate turn on, a ridiculously thick and sexy woman in a tight little skirt, driving an eighteen-wheeler.

"Bae, don't go back to 69. Go to Route 23," Macho told her, wanting to avoid the southbound weight station that he knew was on I-69, and was most definitely open.

"Got it," Yessy agreed, and made her way to find the highway he was speaking of. She found it and got on. Merging in traffic, Yessy flowed through the gears smoothly and got cruising in the middle lane, behind a tanker semi. G-Baby laid in back watching the movie, *Baggage Claim* on her iPhone, while Maliante and Dreams laid with her on the bed.

Macho got onto his phone, logged into his private bank account, and donated a hundred and eighty thousand dollars to a charity for children of incarcerated parents, then the remaining hundred thousand dollars to various animal rescue foundations. Just as he dispersed the last bit, his phone rang. The music cut off as the Bluetooth in the head unit picked it up.

Yessy saw the name of the caller pop on the screen. Before Macho could unpair his phone with the head unit, Yessy reached out and pressed "answer."

Macho looked over at her and shook her head as she gave him a smug smile.

"Yo?" came Narco's voice from the speakers.

"What up, cutty?" Macho asked, turning his eyes back to the road.

"Aye, my nig, you heard?" Narco asked.

"About?"

"Shit went down in the 'Raq. Clown-ass Ecuadorians that was snatchin' and sellin lil' young ass girls got they ass burnt up."

Macho laughed. "Imagine that."

"I can't even lie, bro. When I heard, I was immediately thinkin', that is some shit my nigga Macho would do. Ain't no such thing as a simple ass whoopin', or a bullet to the head."

Macho laughed even harder, while Yessy and G-Baby both curled their lips up in disgust, just at the sound of Narco's voice.

"But then, I'm like naw. Bro wouldn't get involved with some shit that ain't have nothin' to do with him," Narco then said.

"Well, even if it didn't have anything to do with me, per se, if somethin' like that involved my peoples, I would most definitely jump in and get to regulatin'," Macho told him.

Now Narco laughed. "Aw, come on, my nigga. Shit like that, breakin' up a sex traffickin' ring? Bro, muhfuckas in that world are ruthless, you definitely can't get yourself wrapped up in that. Niggas might come for you if they found out it was you that did that shit."

"Well, again, if I had something to do with it, I would welcome anyone that feels gangsta enough to try me. I was born a muthafuckin' tiguere, and I'ma die as one."

Yessy glanced back at G-Baby. She saw her homegirl shake her head, likely thinking the same thing she was thinking.

"Um, excuse me," Yessy cut in just then. "You talkin' real reckless right now on an open line, yo. Don't nobody know what the fuck you talkin' about, so shut that hot shit the fuck up."

They all heard Narco mutter a curse, Macho surmised that he realized he was on speaker, and Macho wasn't the only one listening.

"My bad…ma'am. Uh, I'll let you go, Macho. We still on, though, right? On that move?"

Yessy shot a look over at her man and saw his jaw muscles flexing, as if he was trying to contain frustration.

She spoke again before anyone else could. "What move is this?" she demanded to know, still glaring at Macho.

"A car…for my grandma," Narco told her. "I asked bro if he could pick it up for me so I can give it to her on her b-day."

"Oh really?" Yessy said, again, glancing over at Macho and saw him refusing to look over at her. "What type of present?"

"A 1970 Hemi Cuda…it was getting' restored."

"Why is it that I bet you're going to tell me that it's down in Texas somewhere?" Yessy asked, as she downshifted a gear to slow down even more as traffic slowed to just forty miles an hour.

"Because…that's where my uncle that does car restoration is."

"Okay, well you're gonna have to find another person to go get it, because he is not going," Yessy told Narco, "and I would really appreciate it if you stopped calling my man. I do not like you, nobody does, so leave him thee fuck alone, or I swear on God, I will send you to meet my friend, Heavy B."

Before Narco could respond, Yessy reached out to the head unit and ended the call. Macho shook his head at her.

"Got somethin' to say?" she asked him.

Smiling, G-Baby watched and cheered Yessy on inside her head.

"Nope," Macho said, but was thinking, *you got me fucked up…I'm grown, and I'm goin' down there to pick that shit up…nobody gonna stop me, homiez!*

"Good. Then once we get these cars delivered, we're gonna take a break from this crap and focus on legit biz," Yessy declared. Then she turned the music back up and started singing along with Lil' Wayne's, "Pussy, Money, Weed."

Macho remained quiet, not wanting to argue. He leaned back and looked out of his window, continuing his thoughts on business and money.

Chapter 12

Macho

Just over five hours late, Macho re-entered Illinois. Back onto 90/94, he passed through the Skyway Tool booth, then blew through Chicago. He took the Dan Ryan Expressway, cruising along with the heavy flow of Chi-Town traffic. As he made his way north, Macho's plan to handle the business for the old Arab formed in his head. He couldn't help but smile at the thought of the look on Jamal's face when it all went down.

***

Bone Thugs-N-Harmony's "For The Love of Money," featuring Eazy-E blasted. Macho, Yessy, and G-Baby rapped out loud when Eazy's verse came on.

"Standin' on the corner straight slaaaangin' rocks, aaaawwwwww shit here comes the muthafuckin' cops, so I dash, I ducks, and I—"

Their mode was interrupted when a call from Jamal came in. Pissed, Macho answered it.

"Now, that's three times you fuckin' my mode up, yo! What the fuck do you want?" he snapped.

Yessy and G-Baby busted out laughing.

"Bro! It's almost seven o'clock! Where are you?" Jamal demanded to know.

"I'm up ya' momma's booty hole and around the corner, bitch! Stop fuckin' callin' me. I'll be there very soon!"

Macho ended the call on him. The music came back on and they continued.

"Hide behind a tree! Makin' sure them muthafuckaz don't see me!"

***

From the Dan Ryan, Macho got up to the Kennedy Expressway and switched to it, then took it to Rosemont, where Jamal's new and used car dealership was.

The sun began to set as he made his way up I-90. Once he came upon his exit, he got off and maneuvered El Viejo through the Cook County suburb. Yessy reached up into a small compartment, grabbing a Faraday Bag. She tossed her iPhone in, then Macho and G-Baby put theirs in. The metal-mesh bag killed their GPS signals immediately, making any way to trace their whereabouts impossible. Fifteen minutes later, he arrived at a fence-lined property with a showroom building in the center of it, with foreign and domestic cars parked around on display.

He turned on the jake-brake and down-shifted gears as he approached the entrance. He made a wide right turn in and headed towards the rear, where a storage warehouse was.

Yessy rubbed Dream's head as she looked out the window, peeping around Jamal's property. It wasn't her nor G-Baby's first time there. Other than a few changes to the building, it was all still the same. Yessy found herself a little shocked as she remembered the request made by Jamal's uncle, but no matter what, if her man was about it, then she was, and no doubt that G-Baby was.

Reaching the back of the dealership, Macho saw the candy-orange Hummer H2 on thirty-inch Forgiatos that Jamal owned. Next to it was a red Ferrari 458 Speciale that he'd seen before, and knew was owned by Jamal's right-hand man.

Parked off to the side were three vehicles that Macho hadn't seen there before. The bronze 1970 Chevy Chevelle SS on Rallies was looking pretty damn clean. Parked to its side were two older hot-rod built Ford pick-up trucks.

Macho then saw Jamal and his homie Ahmaan, posted up in front of the warehouse's tall garage door. A few feet to their right, Macho saw seven angry-looking white men.

"They don't look happy," Yessy said, as she turned the music down.

"I wouldn't be either if I was in business with a clown like Jamal," Macho replied.

He made a big U-turn and got El Viejo turned around, lining the rear of the trailer up with the warehouse's door. He put the brakes on, shifted in neutral, then looking at his woman, he nodded his head. "See you in a minute," he said to her.

Yessy nodded. "Love you, baby."

Macho smiled. "Love you, too, gorgeous. Now let's get this Arab money!"

Jamal

Fifteen minutes earlier…

"I'm tired of waitin', Jamal! Where the fuck is this son of a bitch at with my shit?" snapped Country, a tall, bearded man with pale skin, and a bald head.

Jamal was damn near about to shit his pants. His home boy Ahmaan looked terrified as well. The mob of white boys were armed, pissed, and high as hell off crystal meth. There was no telling what they would do if they had to wait another half an hour.

"Relax, Country!" Jamal begged. "I just talked to him! He's close, man!"

"Look here, you little rag head motherfucker! Fuck waiting! If that son of a bitch doesn't get here in three minutes, you and your little insurgent friend are gonna hang!" Country threatened, so ready to end the two young Middle Eastern heroin dealers' lives, take his money back, and find anything of value that he could take back down to Granite City with him and his crew of racist druggies.

Jamal and Ahmaan stayed silent. They were way too afraid to talk back. They were outnumbered, and didn't truly have a gangster bone in their bodies.

"He's coming, Country! Come on, man! Macho always delivers!" Jamal assured the hefty bearded white man.

Standing six feet two inches tall and built like WWE star Brock Lesnar, Country was an intimidating man. Wearing a plain t-shirt, jeans, and cowboy boots, with a bald head, he looked like he lived in a farmhouse and killed people of color for fun.

"Yeah, Country. Macho never balks on business, dude," Ahmaan co-signed with his homie.

Country's eyebrows furrowed at Ahmaan's additional words. He looked over at where his mob of white men stood, each of them with a swastika tatted on them somewhere. He nodded his head at one of them, giving the guy a "get him" gesture.

The crazy-looking guy with dilated pupils walked right up to Ahmaan with a grin and smacked the shit out of him. Ahmaan yelped from the sting. He fell backwards to the floor, rubbing his face.

Jamal gasped when Country pulled out his Smith & Wesson 454 and thumbed back the hammer on the big revolver.

"Country! Come on, man! He's …" Jamal paused mid-sentence when he heard the sound of Macho's super-loud Peterbilt. "He's here! That's him, bro!" he said, relieved beyond belief.

Country told his guys to get the garage door opened up, then he looked out towards the entrance. He saw the old Peterbilt, pulling a car-carrier loaded with cars creeping in his direction.

"That is one spooky-lookin' rig," he said to himself, catching a chill up his spine at the sight of the ancient 359 Extended Hood.

His guys agreed, all of them creeped out by the old truck. They kept their hands close to their waistlines as the rig backed into the garage and stopped in the middle, about thirty or forty feet away from them all. Country began smiling as he looked at the seven cars on the trailer. He was so ready for his heroin. It was his biggest re-up ever.

His guy hit the button and closed the door back. The truck's engine cut off. Country stared at the driver's door. He couldn't see past the tinted glass at all.

"What the hell you waitin' on?" Country shouted at the driver.

The door opened up and he saw a tall and muscular light brown-skinned man, with long braids, a neatly lined beard, and strange colored eyes. He was dressed in a plain t-shirt, slightly baggy jeans, and Timberlands. As he moved to get out, he put on a Pittsburgh fitted.

He grinned as he got out the truck. "What up, Jamal? Mike Mike? Y'all lookin' like y'all a little stressed out."

"Hey!" Country barked. "Close your goddamn mouth and get them damn cars off that trailer! Hurry up!"

Jamal and Michael saw Macho chuckle.

"Yessuh, massa'! I's a gon' get 'dem 'dea 'cahs of dis hea' traila', suh! Yes, I is!" Macho clowned.

***

Just under twenty minutes later, all seven cars were unhooked and parked in a row, facing away from Country and his men. The six guys went in the vehicles' trunks and had pulled out fifty bricks of heroin.

Country saw he was twenty short. He was so furious that he turned almost as red as his beard.

"Where the hell's the other twenty, you son of a bitch?" he snapped, ready to blow Jamal's brains out.

"Y-you paid for f-fifty!" Jamal stammered. "It's fifty-five a brick, bro! You paid twenty-seven and a half, man!"

"You mutherfucker! You said forty K, goddammit! I want my shit right now!"

Country pointed his pistol at Jamal's face. His men took aim at him as well, along with Ahmaan.

"Aye, my man," Macho interrupted, getting Country's attention. "I'm not gon' be able to let you shoot Dumb-Dumb. I gots business to handle with him."

"I don't give a rat's ass what the fuck you got goin' on! Shut your fuckin' mouth, ya' blue eyed ni—"

PFFT! PFFT! PFFT!

PFFT! PFFT! PFFT!

Six heads exploded in less than six seconds. Blood and brains and skull flew all over Country, Jamal, and Michael. Country spun around and saw the bodies of this men on the ground, with pools of blood forming around headless corpses.

"What the hell?" Country shouted, then spinning back towards Macho. "What did you do, ya' son of a bitch?"

"I didn't do shit, mama huevo, but, it did sound like you's gon' call me somethin' that ya' schmuck-ass cocksucker ancestors loved sayin' to people that are waaaaay better than you and them."

"Motherfucker!" Country yelled, then raised up his gun at Macho. He was about to fire, when the swing doors to the main hallway busted open and in ran the same Pit Bull Jamal's ass was almost eaten by, and a big Rottweiler.

"Oh shit!" Country went to run, dropping his gun when the Pit Bull caught him first, jumping up and chomping down on his ass cheek.

The Rottweiler jumped and took Country down to the ground as he screamed in agony from the Red Nose brindle, biting down harder on his cheek. The German killer then sank his teeth into the man's face and ripped the whole left side of his face off.

Jamal and Ahmaan cringed at the sight of all the blood. The agonizing screams coming from such a big man made Macho laugh.

Macho

Laughing so hard that tears filled his eyes, Macho saw his woman and G-Baby come through Jamal's office, where the tall and wide glass window had six bullet holes in it. Slung around their shoulders were .50 caliber H&K semi-auto sniper rifles. Yessy had a machete as well. She took it to her man and gave it to him.

Country bled profusely onto the ground, still screaming after Maliante devoured the meat he'd ripped away from Country's face, and from Dreams still trying to rip his ass cheek off, Macho went towards where Country's revolver was. With his machete in his left hand, Macho grabbed the huge Smith & Wesson with his right. He smirked to himself, then he looked down at Country. He pointed the cannon directly at Country's face and whistled at him.

The man looked up and saw his own gun pointed at him.

"NO!"

POW!

Head was obliterated, in chunks all over the ground. Country's body tensed up as his nerves tightened, then his body went completely limp.

Macho looked at his dog. "Release!" he commanded her.

Obediently, Dreams let go and went to his side with blood smeared all over her muzzle. Maliante went to Yessy's side and sat, but his eyes stayed locked onto Jamal and Ahmaan, as were Dreams.

"Th-thank you, bro!" Jamal stuttered, relief washing over him.

"For?" asked Macho, with a raised eyebrow.

"Dude was gon' pop us all, bro! He crazy as hell!"

"Oh." Macho chuckled. "He's crazy, huh?"

"Yeah, bro! Fuck him, though! I got almost three million and I still got the dope! Ha!"

PFFT!

Ahmaan's head exploded all over Jamal when Yessy pointed her G-series sniper at it and pulled the trigger.

Jamal screamed, covered with more brains and blood.

"What the fuck?" he screeched, seeing his boy on the ground without a head.

Macho raised up the 454 and pointed it at Jamal's face.

"No…no…no! Wait!" he begged, putting his hands up to cover his mug.

"Really? This muhfucka just blew fatboy's head to pieces, you think ya' hands can deflect one of these bullets?"

Yessy and G-Baby chuckled at Macho.

"Wh-what d-d-do you w-want?"

"Where are the diamonds you stole from yo' uncle? Do not lie!" Macho warned, and for emphasis, Yessy went to Jamal and grabbed his head, forcing him to look Macho in his eyes.

Yessy clenched her teeth and growled through them. "You got three seconds to talk!"

He spilled it all. Okay! It's in the safe in my office, man! Just please don't kill me! I got kids, man!"

"Your kids would be better off not havin' such a bitch for a daddy," Macho said, as Yessy and G-Baby shook their heads at Jamal's cowardice. "Lead the way, my friend, and before you try to grab a weapon you may have stashed somewhere close by, think about all the movies where people tried that shit and failed," he added, then raising the machete to Jamal's nose, Macho commanded him to walk.

Chapter 13

Macho followed behind the trembling Arab with his machete in his hand. Yessy followed behind the two, keeping her eyes peeled for any surprises. G-Baby and the dogs headed out of the warehouse and posted up outside of the showroom building, where Jamal's office was. She got back into military mode, pretending that she was back in Iraq, keeping watch over soldiers in her camp.

Two minutes after they entered the building, Jamal opened the door to his lush office and pointed to a big oil painting hanging on his wall.

"How about you stop pointing, go take that wack-ass paintin' down, and show me what's behind it?" Macho suggested.

Jamal got the safe open in one try. As he opened the door, he saw the small caliber pistol, resting on top of a small satin cover. He looked at it.

"Go ahead…go for it," he heard Macho say, right in his right ear. "I dare you."

Jamal shrieked when he felt the end of the machete poking him in his ass crack. He stepped away and saw Macho's smiling like the Grinch.

"Smart man," Macho said before grabbing the little peashooter out of the safe. He pulled away the little satin sheet and his eyes lit up. "Well, well, well…now this is a lick! You see this, bae?"

Yessy peered over and saw shiny gold bars stacked on top of each other. They were not small.

"Maaaan, Macho, why you helpin' my uncle out, man? He owes me millions for all the things I've done for him, bro!" Jamal said, trying to find a way to keep at least some of the gold bars.

"Jamal…shut up," Macho said, looking around the office for something to put the gold in.

The Arab closed his mouth and watched helplessly as Macho found a bookbag. He went and filled the bag with every single gold bar in the safe. The last one, he held it up and looked at it.

"Hmmm……we'll have to look the prices of gold up, bae. These are fifty ounces each," he told Yessy, tossing the last bar in with the others.

Yessy nodded but said nothing. Her focus was still on Jamal, watching him, waiting for him to try something.

"You got the gold, man," Jamal said to Macho. "You're gonna let me live, right?"

Macho grinned at him. "Yes, after you put the dope back in one of the cars for me to take. I will make sure you get a nice vacation, in the warmest place on …in earth."

Yessy snickered when she saw Jamal sigh in relief.

***

Twenty gold bars total went into the book bag. Macho found stacks of cash in another compartment of the safe. He was just about to close the door when his woman halted him. She pointed at another small little door near the bottom corner.

Macho went and opened it and saw a little suede bag inside, tied up with a silver string. He held it up and shook it, holding it close to his ear, hearing something that sounded like pebbles shifting around inside.

Jamal started freaking out. "Macho! No, man, come on! Those aren't mine!"

"Well, now I gotta see what's inside this lovely bag," Macho said, and untied the bag.

The second Macho looked inside, he went wide-eyed. "Holy shit!" he exclaimed and turned to his woman. "Bae! Mira!" he told her.

Yessy walked towards him and looked in the bag. Her eyes lit up like Christmas lights.

"Daaaaayuuuuuuum, this little motherfurcker is holdin' real heavy in this bitch, yo!" she said.

Jamal made a break for it, taking off and running like a bat flying wildly out of hell. He bent the corner and ran like the wind towards the exit doors. He was just a few feet away from freedom when he heard a "pop," then a millisecond later, he felt the most excruciating pain explode in his right ass cheek.

He screamed at the top of his lungs as he went down. Jamal grabbed his obliterated booty cheek and could feel the warm sticky blood pouring out of the gaping wound, made by the slug fired by Yessy when she stepped out of the office and put the beam on his ass.

Macho walked up to where the youngster cried and screamed in agony. He shook his head, looking down at him.

"I'm sorry! I'm sorry!" Jamal begged and bled. "Pleeeeeease! It hurts so baaaad! I need a—"

BOC! BOC! BOC! BOC! BOC! BOC! BOC! BOC! BOC! BOC! BOC! BOC!

Yessy stopped firing when half of Jamal's body was reduced to chunks of bloody meat. She walked up next to her man and smiled at him. He shook his head at her, chuckling at her as well.

"I think I'm going to make it a rule that every time we gots to handle business, you have to wear a skirt," he told her, feeling so incredibly attracted to her, more than he already was.

Yessy laughed, then looked at the corpse. "That's for waking me up, pendejo."

Without a word more, Macho and his woman headed back out with the bag, ready to finish up and get up out of there.

***

Outside, G-Baby stood on security with her sniper with Dreams and Maliante assisting. Parked at the front of the building was Macho's cousin, Javi. He had pulled up in his black Kenworth T800, coupled to a car-carrier trailer identical to the one coupled up to El Viejo.

The five foot eleven, green-eyed Dominican's long hair was braided in a fresh zig-zag design, with his baby hairline, and low-trimmed beard lined up sharply. His golden-brown skin tone was the same as his slightly older cousin's. He looked more like he could be Macho's younger brother, instead of his cousin. Javi was slimmer and athletic, with tattooed arms and chest. The soon-to-be twenty-seven-year-old was the father of two two-year-olds, a son from his Dominican wife Michelle, and a daughter from of his former honey dips.

Javi came to assist in the removal of some cars when Macho called him. With a destination for them already worked out, after Yessy had gotten the keys from the dead racists, Javi got the Chevy Chevelle loaded, then the two pick-ups.

***

"Ready, bae?" Macho asked his woman, once she was up inside of El Viejo.

"Yep. Hit it," she told him, starting the engine up.

Macho hit the button to open the rear exit garage door, With the load back on to the trailer, with the other six, Yessy pulled out of the garage. Macho lit up the road flare and tossed it at the big barrel full of motor oil. He and Yessy had doused the place with anything flammable they could find after they got the cars loaded back up on the trailer.

The oil ignited with the ferocity of a gas-soaked couch. Macho ran out of the garage and jumped up into the passenger's side of El Viejo.

The fire quickly spread and was doing its job, burning everything that would pinpoint Macho, Yessy, and G-Baby being there. Macho had taken the hard drive to the security feed and destroyed it, as well as the system.

Yessy whipped El Viejo around the building and passed Javi's idling truck. She and Macho saw G-Baby was inside with him and the dogs. Javi pulled off and rolled behind Yessy. Luckily, they turned out of the property while no traffic or pedestrians were coming. The second they reached the end of the block, Jamal's building exploded, sending a fireball up into the darkening sky that was so big, anyone within five miles could see it.

Yessy

From Rosemont, Yessy led Javi east to Cicero Avenue then shot south, heading towards Chicago-Midway Airport. When they got in the area, she continued leading until the sign for A & D Custom Inc. came up.

She made a left turn into the auto customizing business and saw Man's white trap van, parked in front of the first of six bays to his hundred-and-thirty-thousand-square-foot garage. At the office's door, Man's black and chromed-out 2013 Ford F150, sitting up on big twenty-eight-inch Forgiatos was sitting next to Destiny's newer emerald-green Porsche Cayenne Turbo.

Yessy rolled past the main building and headed towards the rear, where another big garage sat, the size of an airplane hangar.

Posted up out in front, was the brawny six-foot-one-inch-tall Amir Jones, aka Man. He was a dark-brown-skinned man, sporting a bald-fade, a neat beard. He rocked a short-sleeve polo-style shirt that had A&D Customs, Inc. stitched into the left side of his chest, jeans, and down on his feet, he rocked a pair of Yeezys.

As Yessy pulled up, the door next to Man opened up, and out came his woman Destiny, mother of his almost five-year-old son, Audi. His lookalike son was dressed just like him.

Destiny was a glamorous, high-yellow-skinned chick, standing five feet six inches tall, without the shiny gold Christian Louboutins on her feet. She was looking like a fashion queen in the dark-blue suede top leather bottom Balenciaga dress that fit her very voluptuous body like a second skin. The dark-blue diamond patterned pantyhose accentuated her legs, adding sophistication to her undeniable hood chic swagger. Her long buckwheat-dyed hair was braided in neat plaits and put into a ball on the top of her head. Draped in gold jewelry, with her long nails matching minimal makeup, Destiny was the type of chick that needn't say a word to have men lust for her.

Both she and her man were twenty-five, owners of the big auto-custom business, with other avenues of business bringing in millions of dollars, not including all the cocaine they moved for Macho and his brother.

***

Man pulled out his keys from his pocket and hit a button on one of his fobs. The enormously wide and tall hangar door began flipping up, opening up a view of three long rows of some of the most expensive foreigners and exotics people could get their hands on.

Yessy pulled El Viejo inside, with Javi pulling in right behind her. Man, Destiny, and their son entered as they both parked on a big section outlined in yellow. The door was closed back down as Yessy and Javi cut their engines off.

They all got out of the trucks and were greeted by African American perfection.

***

"Audiii!" Yessy, squealed excitedly, running to the miniature Man, overjoyed to see the little guy again.

"Hi, Auntie Yessy!" Audi excitedly said as she hugged and kissed all over his face.

G-Baby joined in. She too adored Audi, as if he was her son. Macho and Javi hugged Destiny in brotherly embraces, then they dapped Man up.

"My boy! It's good to see you, my nigga," Javi said to Man.

"Been a little bit too long, Joe."

Man chuckled. "Indeed it has. Me and bae just be on bidness, you dig I'm sayin'?"

The guys laughed at how Destiny twisted her lips up at the two. Macho was then hit with the memory of how he and Yessy met Man and Destiny at a restaurant in Zion, after drinks. Macho and Yessy wouldn't be alive if it weren't for them.

***

Exiting the restaurant, Man, walking with his woman, saw the van ride past them. The headlights were off, and he was able to catch a glimpse of the masked-up driver through the window. He looked ahead and saw the man and woman walking towards a row of cars, laughing and enjoying their own evening. Man had seen the two love birds inside, eating and sipping. He had inadvertently connected with the two, seeing himself and his woman in them. But he had also peeped a couple of Latinos by the bar that seemed to be watching the two.

Outside the restaurant, when Man saw the van creeping towards the two, he reacted. Destiny, picking up on his mood change, saw the van and knew what her man was on. They both hurried to their vehicle and grabbed their semi-automatic pistols that were stashed under their seats, then they took off running towards the van, just as it screeched to a stop just feet away from Macho and Yessy.

The mob hopped out with choppers and diabolical smirks. Instinctively, Macho pulled his lady behind him, ready to shield her with his life, when suddenly gunshots rang out that were not from the Sicarios.

Two heads exploded and four others, after attempting to point their assault rifles in the direction of where the shots were coming from, took slugs to their chest and faces. The last two tried to shoot, but Macho had run up on one of them, grabbed him and broke the man's neck with his hands. Yessy got the last one with the knife she had in her handbag. She jabbed him in the back of his head, penetrating his brain, killing him instantly.

Macho and Yessy were beyond grateful to the two, but there was no time to express gratitude with words.

"Go! Y'all gotta bounce! There could be more!" Man had told them as he and his woman prepared to get out of there themselves.

Macho quickly got his woman into his BMW but was able to get the license plate number on Man's Mercedes when he peeled off with Destiny.

Days later, Macho and his woman popped up on Man and Destiny at their home, with Macho's cousin, grandfather, grandmother, and ChaCha. Man and Destiny were shocked speechless when they saw the group in front of their house. Macho used his connects to find out where they lived, then paid them a visit to make sure to officially extend his gratitude for risking their lives and freedom, to save his woman and himself.

To say the least, that day, Man and Destiny had become a part of the Valdez family. They had wanted for nothing ever again and got the plug. Grade-A cocaine that made them so much money, they built themselves a few of their own businesses that turned their bank account statements into what looked like phone numbers.

***

"Here y'all go with that shit again," Destiny said with a laugh. "Don't make me come up outta my Red Bottoms in front of my son."

"Uh huh, I hear that hot shit you poppin', son… but by the time one heel comes off, you'll be on that big ol' booty you got," Yessy replied, giving Destiny a taunting smile.

"Auntie Yessy! Mommy's pregnant!" Audi then said, looking geeked all the way up about it.

Yessy and G-Baby gasped and looked at Destiny. They both screamed with excitement and ran to her.

"Oh my God! Congratulations, sis! Damn, yo! You 'bout to have number two and I haven't even had my first yet! Slow down a little bit!" Yessy joked.

"Guuuurl, don't blame me," Destiny said, then she shot a look in the direction where her man, Macho, and Javi were talking amongst each other.

Yessy and G-Baby busted out laughing. G-Baby's eyes then landed on a few cars that instantly caught her attention.

"Oh shit! How did y'all get y'all hands on a GT40?" she asked in shock, knowing how rare the black and bronze 1966 Ford racing car was.

"That's Macho's car, this whole row is," Destiny said. Yessy looked at an even rarer Mercedes-Benz SLK GRT LeMans racer, jaw dropping to the floor. She marched right over to her man, interrupting his conversation.

"Why don't I know about these cars bein' yours, Antonio?"

Man, Destiny and Javi busted out laughing.

"I forgot I had them, bae," he told her, taking a step back.

"Anything else you forgot to tell me you have, asshole?" she asked.

"I might have a yacht, and a mansion in Miami, but definitely an empty stomach. So how about we get these cars unloaded and get back. I am starving!"

***

All the cars were unloaded from the trailer, and after Macho showed Man the contents of the Benz, Man immediately made calls to his black boys to come eat.

"What you need back for these joints, family?" Man asked, as Yessy and G-Baby got the trailers ready to go.

"Bro, them yours, do you. That shit was free for me, so it's free for you," Macho said.

"You've been wantin' to expand anyways," chimes in Javi. "Not that you ain't already have it, but no, you got more capital, and the best backers in the Midwest to help whoever and however we can."

Man nodded his head, grateful for the two. "Fa'sho. Me and bae gon' shoot some ideas around, we been thinkin' of startin' a business where we customize jets and helicopters. Des' been wantin' to dive into interior designin' for houses."

"Go for it," said Yessy, as she and G-Baby walked up. "Forget just thinking about it, Amir. Dreams stay dreams unless you make them happen, 'yah mean?"

"True." Man nodded his head.

Macho smiled and laughed.

"What?" Yessy asked with a raised eyebrow.

"I could write an urban novel about the two of them, yo. I would call it *Destiny's Man*, and that shit would be fly as hell!"

They all started laughing at Macho, but the idea didn't sound bad at all to Yessy and G-Baby.

"Whoa! Aye! Check it out!" G-Baby handed her phone to Yessy, who was in the passenger's seat. "Prices of gold per ounce! There's twenty, fifty-ounce bars in the bag, sis!"

Macho smiled to himself as he ascended the on-ramp to the E-way. He already knew the price, which was at an all-time high for the season.

"Oh, damn… thirteen hundred and fifty dollars per ounce?" Yessy saw, attempting to do the math in her head.

"Woooooow. Dude's uncle wants it back, though right?" Yessy asked.

"Bae, Mr. Hasan was Jamal's plug's plug." He glanced over at her with a grin. "That man is as rich as a Saudi Arabian oil tycoon. The hit he put on Jamal was paid for by the diamonds and gold."

"Okay, then! Shit! So…what's going to come of it all?" she asked, looking over at him as he cruised with one hand on the wheel.

"I have an idea in mind and if Michelle can do it, we are gonna have happiest drivers ever!" Macho told her.

***

Macho

Arriving back at the Valdez Transport yard, Macho turned in, with Javi behind him. They backed Evelyn's car-hauler trailers into her section of the yard, where a few of her twin-car transport rigs now were, after an early start, and early finish. All of Xavier's heavy-haul trucks were back, as were all of the trucks and trailers in Javi's intermodal/dry-van freight crew.

As the two cousins got out to uncouple from the car-haulers, Evelyn's bit 880 Volvo rolled into the yard, followed by Nena in her Peterbilt 389. Right behind the two luxury auto-trailers, was the nearly half-million Brabus-edition

Mercedes G65 AMG, rolling on twenty-four-inch Forgiatos that matched the wine-colored SUV's paint.

While Evelyn and Nena went and got their rigs backed into their spots, the V12-powered G-Wagon came to a stop in front of Javi's truck.

The driver's door opened up a second later. Out came Javi's beautiful twenty-eight-year-old wife Michelle, dressed in a tight leather Fendi dress and heels. Her long dark-brown hair was up in a flower-bud bun, with two bangs hanging down, encircling her exotic face.

She was a brown-sugar-complexioned woman standing in all aspects of the word. Outshining all her diamond jewelry, which she had custom designed herself, the big pink eight-carat Harry Winston diamond ring on her finger sparkled, since the day Javi had put it on her finger close to two years ago.

Born and raised in Manhattan, New York's Washington Heights neighborhood, Michelle was straight from the hood. She was as ambitious as any woman with a purpose in life, and she was selfless to a fault. Her selflessness was how she became a contract killer, avenging her best friends, whom had been raped and murdered by the neighborhood creep.

Now, as a mother, and owner of her own diamond jewelry design business, Michelle was all the way up. She had her own cake, but being married to a handsome green-eyed highway kingpin, she barely ever got to spend a dime of her own money.

***

"Yeeeeooooo, tiguerasooooo!" shouted Michelle, seeing her favorite cousin-in-law.

"New Yitty in this biatch!" Macho hollered back, hugging Michelle emphatically. "Whaz hamin, lil cuz?"

Before she could respond he heard, "Machoooo!" hollered from the G-Wagon.

"Uh-oh! The monsters are here! Run! They gonna' get us!" Macho played, creeping towards the rear driver's side door of Michelle's SUV. He opened the door, and saw his cousin's minute two-year-old son, Javi Jr. in the car seat behind his mother's seat, and Javi's little brown-skinned daughter Amara, also two years old, in the car seat next to her big brother. Javi and Michelle's Cane Corso, Demon laid at their feet, and his pregnant mate, Diamond, sitting on the front seat. "Oh, noo! The monsters! Somebody help me before they catch mee!"

Javi Jr. and Amara laughed at him so hard. Yessy, G-Baby both could hear them. Their hearts were warmed by how good Macho was with children. The two little ones loved him to death.

While Javi Jr. was the product of Javi and Michelle, Amara was not. She was Javi's daughter, born into the world by a jump-off that he was fucking around with on the side. It ended horribly when Javi was found with a knife in his chest, after attempting to confront Angela about her slick mouth.

His sister Evelyn and her crew of lady auto-haulers were the ones to catch Angela when she attempted to flee the country. Macho had lent a hand, but right as Evelyn was about to blow her head off in the middle of a busy street in broad daylight, the revelation of her claiming to be pregnant with Javi's child, had him make his youngest cousin pump her brakes.

Soon after, Angela was confirmed to be pregnant, and was held in a mansion, for her to give birth…at least it was the plan. Michelle let her go, and despite having been the main one that wanted her dead, she gave her enough money to be cool for a very long time.

Amara was born months later. Angela hadn't been seen since being let go. Then one day, an intruder-alert popped up on Javi's and Michelle's phones. They thought beef had found its way to their new home and ran to greet it head on, only to discover the infant girl in a basket at the front door, by herself. Angela had disappeared. Nobody knew where she went, but almost everyone was sure that she was dead and had their suspicions of who did it.

***

Yessy grabbed the bookbag from El Viejo and took it to Michelle. Evelyn and Nena came up and joined in, greeting kids and the dogs, then listening to Macho's use on what he saw the gold and diamonds being turned into.

Michelle busted out laughing. "Yo cuz, you dun' watched *State Property* too many times, B!"

Javi couldn't help but chuckle himself. "I can't even lie, cuz, that shit would be dope as fuck. I don't think I ever saw that before?"

Macho grinned. "You haven't, but when la tiguerasa de la Heights makes it happen, you will. And don't be tryna bite my idea neither, nigga."

Javi twisted up his lip. "I'll come up with somethin' better, fam. Watch 'n see."

Macho waved it off. "Whatever, lil dude. Get at me, I'm tired, hungry and ready to turn my brain off for a week. Mujeres, let's ride."

Yessy, and G-Baby hugged Michelle, Javi, the kids, then Evelyn and Nena. They got Dreams and Maliante back up in the ol' school Pete and Macho pulled off, roaring towards the exit.

Chapter 14

Notorious B.I.G.'s "Notorious Thugs," featuring Bone Thugs-n-Harmony, pounded from the system as Macho cruised south on Green Bay Road. In the sleeper with the dogs, G-Baby rapped along with the chorus, while Yessy silently mouthed the words.

Coming upon where 9th Street crossed Green Bay Road, his eyes went wide when a black Lincoln Navigator suddenly pulled out from 9th and stopped in the middle of the four-way.

"Que carajo?" Macho cursed, slamming on the brakes trying to stop his bob-tail tractor at sixty miles an hour to zero in seconds, with no weight on the rear to keep the wheels from skidding.

Yessy and G-Baby flew forward off the bed and hit the floor. Dreams and Maliante started barking, already sensing something was wrong.

"Hijuey puta! What the fuck is you doing, dumbass?" Macho shouted, after coming to a stop, feet away from hitting the SUV's passenger side.

His goon instincts kicked in a milli-second after, as did Yessy's and G-Baby's. They hurried to grab a gun from the multiple hideaway gun racks, Dreams and Maliante were both ready to put in some work.

The Navigator's doors opened up just then. The second Macho saw who was getting out of the rear passenger's side, he cursed under his breath.

Yessy and G-Baby saw her and immediately raised their Sig Sauer MPXs to shoot.

"Stop," Macho said to them, which made them look at him incredulously. "You know out of everyone we could put down…she is off limits."

Yessy curled her lip up in disgust. "I should smack the fuck outta you right now, yo."

"Me, too, Charlatan," G-Baby said, as the woman in the sexy officer chick attire and high-heels, joined by four men in black suits, made their way towards Macho's door.

***

Agent Roxanne Bermudez

Roxanne was five foot seven-inches tall, had a beautiful Cuban caramel-brown skin tone, with long silky hair, dark at the roots, but turned blondish gold to the curled ends. She was athletic, petite, with a perfectly symmetrical set of breasts, with a cleavage that the silk blouse to the tight-fitting skirt suit allowed to be seen. The black dotted pantyhose she wore, added to her officially sexy attire, as did her shiny five-inch pointed toe pumps.

The thirty-year-old Latina was bad, and she was mad, eager to grab the big bulky cocaine trafficking goon out of his spooky old truck and slap her cuffs on him. But couldn't.

During a brief undercover operation that her boss had put her on, soon after being recruited into the Drug Enforcement Agency, right out of the Waukegan Police Department, her target had put the woo on her. His dreamy bedroom blues, his flawless tattooed golden-brown skin, and his muscles had made her compromise her mission, for the chance to fuck the ridiculously rich and powerful Macho Valdez. And right after he made her cum three times in a row…she learned that what she thought was a hot and passionate encounter, was a recorded set-up, which landed her behind a desk for almost a year, when her boss found out about it.

Back in the field now, after proving herself to her boss, Roxanne had been put in charge of her own task force, targeting big drug distributors around Illinois. Weeks ago, an uptick in overdose deaths from hot batches of cocaine had caught her attention. She had sent in many agents to go undercover. The reports all came back the same.

Someone was cutting the cocaine in the ILL-state with a dangerous additive that was so lethal that just touching it could kill.

Roxanne had raided many cartel stash spots and trap houses belonging to gangs. A few soft-hearted individuals sang like Beyonce to get themselves out of a lengthy federal prison sentence. The second Agent Bermudez heard the one name she had been dying to get her revenge on…she got her three most seasoned agents together and headed out to go have a chat with the one called El Tiguere.

***

Her heels clacked on the asphalt as she walked up to the old Peterbilt's driver's door. She could hear the dogs inside, barking and growling viciously.

Coming to a stop a few feet from the door, she looked up and saw him, through the open window. He was looking right at her, and even with fire in them, his bedroom blues sent jolts of excitement shooting throughout her entire body.

Then she saw his wild Puerto Rican girlfriend place herself on his lap, giving her a smug ass smile that made the Cubana want to shoot her teeth out.

"There a problem, Officer?" he asked, in the most sarcastic way ever.

"It's Agent, dickhead!" she snapped at him.

"Oh, my bad, Agent Dickhead."

His girlfriend laughed, as did someone else inside of the truck.

"Still got a slick tongue, I see, Mr. Valdez. You still using it to woo any woman you meet?" she asked and cast his girlfriend a snide smile.

"I know not what you speak of, Agent Dickhead, but I am so hungry at the moment, and your little traffic stop is stopping me from a big juicy burger. So can you please state your reason for blocking the road so I can go?"

"What makes you think you're not under arrest, sir?" Roxanne asked, studying his face, ignoring the glare that his woman was giving him.

"Because I'd already be in cuffs, traga."

Roxanne grinded her teeth in anger when he called her a swallower. His woman's glare turned into a smirk.

"Mamabicho!" came the shout of a woman inside the rig.

Macho and his woman laughed.

"Go ahead and laugh," Roxanne said, with a smirk.

"Let's see how funny it is when Pancho's people come after you."

"Who?" Macho asked, with a raised eyebrow.

"Play stupid if you want, cabrón," she dared.

"Ya mama's a cabrón, bitch," he shot back.

His woman laughed her ass off.

Roxanne so badly wanted to pretend she saw a gun in the girl's hand and pop her.

"I have a suggestion for you, Mr. Valdez," she then said.

"Next time yo' mama comes over to my crib, wear a condom…I know…you don't gotta say it, Agent Dickhead."

Roxanne saw red. "My mother is dead, asshole!"

"Wow! Mine is too! How much you wanna bet that *my* raise'll beat your mother's ass and boot her ass out of Heaven?"

"Valdez! Shut the fuck up, goddammit!" Roxanne screamed.

"Ya' mama's a goddammit, goddammit."

The ladies in the truck were laughing hysterically. Roxanne heard a snicker come from behind her. She turned around and saw one of her agents trying to hold in his laughter.

"Take your ass back to the truck," she ordered.

"Aye, homie! Don't trip, yo! All you gotta do is pull ya' dick out and she'll hop on it!" Macho hollered out to him.

Roxanne turned her head back to Macho.

"There's a lot of bad cocaine on the streets right now, Mr. Valdez. I am going to make it my life's mission to tie it all to you and put you under the Terre Haute."

"Okay, well you have fun with that. Is that all, Agent Dickhead?"

Roxanne smirked at him. "For now," she replied, then turned on her heels to head back to her vehicle. "I will see you soon…asshole."

"Ya' mama's an asshole!" She heard him shout to her.

Macho

He watched the gorgeous DEA agent walk off angrily. Though he couldn't care less about her, Macho couldn't help but to remember how good her juicy lips felt when they were wrapped around his cock, and how tight and wet the pussy was. She even let him fuck her in her ass when they got scummy drunk. The whole time he knew she was a cop. The chick had forgotten that her social media sites were not made private. Anyone with an Instagram could see photos of her in uniform, and even the day she signed on with the DEA.

He played her game, got the pussy and sent her boss the porno flick she had unknowingly went super wild on, ending it with cum all over her face.

***

“Um…hello? Earth to Antonio.” Yessy door-knocked on his forehead, as he watched the agents get back into the SUV.

He came out of his reminiscent daze and looked at her.

“Any chance you can stop reliving that bogus-ass fantasy you had with that bitch while me and Gabi was in Afghanistan, and go?”

The Navigator peeled off and shot around El Viejo heading north. Macho reached around his woman and grabbed the shifter, clutching into gear to roll off.

Yessy went to move as Macho started driving again. But he stopped her, keeping her on his lap. Yessy looked at him as he shifted into 4th. He glanced at her and smiled. She felt his dick growing hard under her. She smiled back at him.

“Maybe we could skip that big juicy burger and go straight to the garage?” she asked, as they came upon their subdivision, passing the entrance seconds later.

“Heeeell no.” Macho shook his head at her suggestion which made her jaw drop. “I really am starvin’, Yessy. I’m finna stop at the Chinese food spot around the corner from here,” he said, coming up on Green Bay Road and Route 173. “Get some General Tso's Chicken and fried rice, with egg rolls, then we can go to the garage and disappear in my office.”

G-Baby

God, I need a man. Why can’t a handsome buff ass nigga like Macho come into my life? she thought, as Yessy giggled while sitting on top of her man’s lap, while he hit a left onto 173.

The rest of the ride to the Chinese food joint and then to the garage, G-Baby remained silent. She tried so hard to stop picturing herself with Macho, naked and sweaty after going at it. Visualizing him putting it on her, the way she always heard him putting it on Yessy, had G-Baby feeling the need to get far away from him, as fast as she could.

Yessinia

"Ooooooo, Antoniooooooo! Baaaeeee!" she screamed out as Macho hit her off.

Yessy was bent over his desk. Behind her, he had her skirt up, and his dick in her asshole. Girl talk made her a big fan of anal sex. Anything hot and dirty, she was all for. Macho loved hitting her in her big phat booty, watching her cheeks bounce and look like they were filled with gelatin.

"Fuck, fuck fuck fuck fuuuuuuuck!" he groaned out. "I finna b-b-buss!"

Yessy had just reached her fourth orgasm before he put it in her ass. Hearing his announcement, she hurried up and pulled him out, then she spun and dropped down, opening her mouth wide, sticking her tongue out. Macho grabbed his dick and put it in her mouth. He grabbed her head and stared in her face, hitting her tonsils every time he went in. Yessy reached up under him, and with one hand she massaged his balls, adding to his pleasure.

Seconds later, he roared and came so hard that his knees nearly gave out. He managed to stay on his feet as he filled her mouth with hot globs of cum. Yessy swallowed it all, then looked up at him with a smile.

"¿Te gusta eso, papi?" she asked him, holding his softening cock in her hand.

"I fucking loved it, mamita," he told her, "and I love you!"

Yessy planted a kiss on the tip of his dick, then he reached down, pulled her up and backing her up against a metal cabinet, he tongued her down until she became putty in his arms. He kissed her for what seemed like a lifetime. Yessy couldn't think of another place she would rather be than with the love of her life, sandwiched in between a cabinet, and his hot, rock-hard body.

His iPhone started dinging. He ignored it at first, then when it started ringing, he pulled back. Yessy licked her lips, savoring his taste and watched lustfully as he went to get his phone from his pocket.

"It's ChaCha," he said, then answered on speaker. "Hablame, prima," he spoke out, walking back towards his woman.

"Oye, papacita, I sent you a video. Check it out," ChaCha told him, then the call ended.

Yessy grew excited when Macho clicked on the video feed link ChaCha sent him. They both knew what it was.

"Pancho versus Heavy B," Macho said with a chuckle. "I wonder who will win?"

"My money is not on Bitch-cho," Yessy said.

Macho brought the link up and clicked play. The video clip filled the screen of his iPhone up, then started playing. They both saw Pancho, face swollen and bloody, compliments of a Rastafarian beat down. He was in a large circular area, surrounded by tall concrete walls. Above it, with a metal screen that allowed sunlight and air in, but nothing to get out.

They could hear Pancho whimpering as he looked around frantically, trying to find a way out of what looked like a big fish tank without water, to him.

"Hey! Somebody, where the fuck am I?" he asked, wiping sweat away that poured from his face. "It's hot as fuck! Let me the fuck outta here!"

"The Motherland is very hot, my man," Macho said, knowing that Pancho had no clue that he was in Nigeria, where his family owned a wildlife reserve, close to where Chloe was from.

Yessy giggled as Pancho started limping around the room, desperate to find a way out. All that was there was a tall and wide steel door. He started banging on it, yelling and demanding to be let out.

"Might not want to do that, yo," Yessy said, dying to see the look on Pancho's face when the door was opened up.

"Aye! Open up! Let me out! Y'all muhfuckas got me bent, Joe!" Pancho yelled, still banging on the door.

Macho and Yessy then heard a voice come out of a loudspeaker.

"Shut up, beetch!"

Macho and Yessy busted out laughing when they heard Asagai's voice.

They saw Pancho turn around and flick off wherever the voice came from.

"Ya momma, beetch," Asagai shouted.

"Is that you, Heavy B? Bring yo' bitchass out here! I'ma beat the fuck out cho' fat ass, then I'ma go home and get all my guys here to murder yo family, bitch! Vamanos, puto," Pancho yelled.

They heard Asagai laugh at him. "Ya wan' fight, eh? A right beetch, here I come!"

Macho and Yessy started grinning in anticipation. The camera zoomed out a little so that they could see Pancho and the door.

It began rising slowly. Pancho turned and looked in the direction. Despite how beat up and in pain he was, he balled his fists up and got ready to fight. Macho shook his head at the poor stupid fool as the door continued raising up.

"This dude really has no clue what' about to happen to him, yo," he said.

Yessy's grin was not a demonic smirk. She was as giddy as a crack fiend that was about to take the first blast of the morning.

"Come on, bitch! I'm ready! I'm from Chiraq! Ain't no bitch in my blood, Heavy B!" Pancho yelled, just as the door reached the very top and stopped.

Beyond the door was total darkness. Pancho stood in boxing form, ready to throw hands, when suddenly he heard what sounded like snorting and grunting.

"Heavy B, baaaabeeeyyyyy!" Yessy cheered.

Macho stayed silent and watched as Pancho took a few steps forward, towards the darkness, He again hollered for Heavy B to come out and fight.

The snorting and grunting got louder. Pancho took four steps back, then his eyes went wide in fear, when he saw the massive four-thousand-pound male hippopotamus come out from the cut, with his eyes locked onto him.

"Oh, shit! Aye! No!" Pancho shouted in fear. "Somebody, heeeeelp!"

Macho and Yessy laughed their asses off. They could hear Asagai laughing as well.

"Muddafucka! Talk dat shit now, beetch! Ya cannot beat an African hippo, muddafucka!"

"Ya better run for it, Pancho!" Yessy said.

Pancho screamed when Heavy B charged him. He attempted to run, but his severely damaged leg, and his sore ass worked against him.

"No! No! No! No! Noooooooo! Noooooooo!" he cried as the hippo got right up on him, his gigantic mouth wide open, revealing long tusk-like teeth.

Macho and Yessy watched as Heavy B caught the Ecuadorian and chomped down on him as hard as he could. Pancho's cries became gags as the powerful jaws squeezed him. His long teeth impaled Pancho like sharp bamboo stalks stabbing right through him. Heavy B shook Pancho around, flailing him like a Pit Bull waving around a chew toy rope.

Seconds later, when he opened his mouth and Pancho went flying, he smacked hard into the wall, then dropped the ground, broken up and in the worst agony a human could experience.

He looked up and saw the hippo coming for him. He tried to move, but his body was broken. Pancho screamed as two tons of angry hippo reached where he lay. Macho and Yessy watched as Heavy B silenced Pancho forever when he laid his body down on the Ecuadorian, smashing him like a pancake.

"Eeww, shit!" Yessy cringed when she and Macho heard Pancho being crushed like a big fat cockroach under a pair of boots.

"Goddamn, bae. Heavy B is a savage." Macho laughed. "The world's number one killer, that can't ever catch a murder charge."

They saw Heavy B get back up on his feet, pieces of smashed Pancho stuck to his side. He trotted off then, heading for the doorway to leave out, to go back to his big lake and submerge himself, until the next time he was needed.

"Wow…that never gets old," Macho said, as the video clip self-deleted completely from his phone.

"Never," Yessy said, "and the day your so-called homie gets to meet Heavy B, I'm gonna watch his fat ass die a hunnid times before I let the video delete, then I'ma laugh my ass off!"

Macho looked at his woman with a raised eyebrow.

"Chinese food, sex, and watchin' Heavy B work and you still plottin' on Narco? What is wrong with you, Yessy?"

"The same thing that's been wrong with me. I hate snake ass niggaz that think they're slick!" Yessy V8 bopped Macho's forehead with her open hand. "And I can't stand how you refuse to listen to any of us about him."

"Cause I don't wanna' hear that bullshit."

Yessy shook her head. She wanted to smack the shit out of him, but she knew that her man was one of the most bullheaded Scorpios on earth.

"Can we go home now? I need some sleep so I can be rested for my shift tomorrow."

Macho sighed. "Yeah, bae. Let's get Gabi and get home."

***

Yessy turned into their driveway twenty minutes later and parked her G-Wagon on the same side as her Maybach. They all headed inside, G-Baby immediately rushing off to her room. Macho fed the caimans while Yessy fed the dogs. Macho then surprised her when he scooped her up off her feet.

"I love you, Yessinia. You know that, right?" he asked, gazing deeply into her eyes.

"I do, baby. You make me so mad sometimes, though."

"Not on purpose. How 'bout I show you how sorry I am up in our bedroom? And I mean really show you over and over again, until you feel like your legs don't work."

"Hmmm…that's gonna take a lot. You think you still got it in you?"

Macho smiled at her. "Only one way to find out, amor."

***

Rico Loves' "They Don't Know" played as he got her on the bed. In seconds, he stripped her naked, then himself. Yessy gazed at him. She was so hot and so ready for him to go crazy on her. She knew she should be getting some sleep, but when it came to getting it on, she could not resist him.

Macho paused and drank in the sight of his woman. "Diablos, amor," he said, shaking his head. "I gotta give it to Big Homie up in the sky, when he created you, he created perfection."

"Aww! Baby!" Yessy said, so full of emotion from his words, making her eyes well up with tears. "I love you so effing much!" she added, just as Wayne Wonder's "No Letting Go" came on.

"Y tambien, yo te amo mucho, bebe," he told her back, then climbed on top of her ready to make love to her under the stars, until they ran out of gas and passed out in each other's arms.

Chapter 15

"Mmmmmm…damn, baby this pussy so good," he groaned as he grinded on her, sliding in and out of her tight wet warm pussy. His eyes rolled to the back of his head as he was overwhelmed by how good she felt around him. "Fuck why did we take so long to do this?" he asked. She moaned, stammering over her words.

"I d-don't kn-know! But sh-sh…stop talking and f-f-fuck me!" she demanded as he filled her with all ten inches of him.

He obliged and started going hard on her, pounding her box like she was his drum. He jackhammered her relentlessly. She wrapped her legs around him, trapping him with her thick thighs. She wasn't letting him go anywhere, even after they both came.

"Shit, Antonio! Oh, God, yes! I been wanting this dick for so long, papi!" she told him as he started going even faster.

"And I been wantin' this pussy for so long, ma," Macho groaned as he hit the bottom of her pussy. "It's mine now, baby."

"Oohhh, shiiiiiiit!" she cried, feeling herself ready to cum. "Aayy, Dios Mio, me voy a venir! Oh my God!"

Macho went even harder on her. He wrapped a hand around her throat and started choking her, enough to where she felt it but not enough to make her pass out. Her whole body began trembling. Her back arched up off the bed and her toes curled up so much that they felt like they would break off. Seconds later, she cried out at the tops of her lungs and came, drenching him with her hot juices. Macho kept stroking her until he reached his own nut. When he came, he roared animalistically. He planted his seed deep inside of her.

"Shit! Goddamn!" he cursed, laying down on top of her.

"Holy shit," she panted, sweaty and tired but feeling so incredibly satisfied. "Coño, papi! I knew you had that bomb, by the way she be screaming her head off while you hitting it, but damn! I have never cum that hard before!"

He chuckled at her. "That's because you ain't never let me hit it before until now."

She giggled. "Just make sure you hit this wet toto at least once a day," she requested, then she reached up and kissed his lips. "I love you, Antonio," she then revealed, looking up into his dreamy eyes.

He smiled back at her, gazing down into her sparkling browns. "I love you too…Gabriela."

Macho

Macho's eyes popped open, then he shot up from off the soft satin pillow. He looked around and saw that he was in his bed.

Goddamit. This shit has to stop! *Why am I dreaming about her again*? he wondered to himself, hating how he had been lusting after G-Baby so hard lately.

He had feelings for her. He tried to chalk it up to just being because he cared for her as his best friend, but it was harder and harder lately to deny that he wanted her…badly! He always had, but now, he found that he just couldn't stop fantasizing about her. He felt nervous and excited when he was around her. She was so fucking beautiful and thick and a straight-up goon. She was just like his woman, and to him, his woman was the epitome of a warrior princess.

***

Macho relaxed on his bed, laying back in just a pair of boxers and Nike basketball shorts. On the giant HDTV, he was watching 50 Cent's *Power*. James and Tommy had become at odds with each other over Angie, James' Puerto Rican jump-off that happened to be on the federal side of the law. The feds were trying to find out who Ghost was, not knowing that James, was Ghost, head honcho of a whole underworld of drugs, guns, and crime.

As he watched, he got a text from Evelyn. *Got something I need to talk to you about. Get at me ASAP. I'll be home.*

Macho typed a reply and told her he'd be out her way in a bit. He saw he had some emails from a few of the owner operator truckers signed on with him. They owned their own trucks and trailers but had no authority to get their own loads. Macho contacted them to haul freight under his company name, for twenty percent of the negotiated fee to haul whatever needed delivered, and he put them as nothing but the highest dollar loads he could find.

Load delivered emails were waiting for him. He opened them and forwarded them to the factoring company he used to get paid upon delivery of freight minus their small fee. He sent payments of his own money to each of the drivers, including a big bonus.

Right as he was about to put his phone back down, he got a video message. He frowned when he saw her number with the video clip.

"What the fuck this bitch want?" he asked himself, hesitating on opening the video. Just as he was about to hit play, Dreams and Maliante ran into the room and jumped up onto the bed, excitedly, dancing and prancing around Macho.

"Here y'all go," he chuckled, as they grunted and snorted at him. "If this lil' shmutt don't leave me alone, I'm a let y'all eat her, okay?" He held up his phone and showed the dogs the picture of the brown-skinned Mexican chick on the screen.

Macho hit play and watched as a wet pussy came onto the screen. He shook his head but continued watching as the pussy's owner started playing with her clit.

"Mmmmmmm…ay, papi…this should be your panocha to be playing with…ven y cojeme como lo hicistes antes. Antonio…yo quiero que tu me cojas comoe tu hicistes la otra semana," he heard Nayeli moan, as those fingers got wetter and wetter.

Macho's eyes were glued to the screen now. He couldn't stop looking. He knew all too well how good the pussy felt, and the throat for that matter. The other week, Macho had royally screwed up and broke the code. He and Yessy got into an argument, and he dipped off, up to Milwaukee hiding out at Narco's house. He initially just went up there to give himself and his woman some space, but after going to a wild party at one of Narco's Kings homie's cribs, Macho ran into Nayeli. There was liquor, she was bad as hell, and that was all that was needed for them to end up naked. The worst part, though, was that Nayeli was Narco's younger sister.

Nayeli's moans got louder and louder, as she brought herself closer to climaxing. Macho swore she was about to start a fire between her legs from how fast she was stroking her clit. He was stuck, though. His dick grew so hard as he remembered how good her pussy felt when he was in it. He even remembered how fresh she tasted the one time he actually ate her out.

Nayeli started moaning his name. He could see her trembling. Seconds later, she exploded. Her juices squired all over the camera lens. It then moved to focus in on her gorgeous face, then exasperatedly, she spoke out to him. "Te extraño mucho, bebe. I want to see you. Don't make me come find you," she said, then she blew him a kiss.

"I do not give a fuck if you miss me, and if you come looking for me…you will likely regret it," Macho said to himself, then shaking his head, he added. "This bitch be tweakin' hard, yo."

He deleted the video and went to send his woman a text so freaky he knew that when she read it, Yessy was likely going to come home and jump him on sight.

"Aye, my man?"

Macho heard that sexy raspy Keyshia Cole voice as he hit "send." He looked towards the doorway and saw G-Baby, in work out apparel. His heart started speeding up when he laid eyes on the unbelievably bad Chicagorilla.

God? Why must you tempt me with her? That shit is not fair, yo. Homiez, yo' ass bogus as hell for how good she looks, Macho thought.

Her hair was up in a bun and she wore a tight purple Fabletics sports bra top that matched the leggings that emphasized the shape of her lower half. Macho's eyes went from her beautiful face to her succulent breasts, her flat stomach, wide hips, thick thighs, her runner's legs, down to her Nike Cross-trained feet. G-Baby looked like she was ready to run from Zion, down to Chicago.

If it wasn't a thick chick in a short skirt, tight dress with sexy panty hose and stilettos that got Macho in hump mode, it was a thick chick in skin-tight work out apparel. Fabletics made every woman that wore the brand look so damn good.

"Uh…um ...hi…whazzup'?" Macho asked as G-Baby walked up to the side of his bed and looked him in his eyes.

"What up? I'm ready for you," she said to him.

Macho's jaw dropped. "Wh-What?"

"Are we gonna' workout still?" G-baby asked, with furrowed brows, reaching out to pat Dream's head.

"Oh! Uh…yeah…we can…do that. Yup," he stammered, kicking himself for thinking it even possible for her to be speaking about fucking.

G-Baby's eyebrow rose up. "Are you okay?"

He nodded. "Yeah up. I am Gucci. Let's…uh…go exercise 'n shit."

G-Baby kissed Dreams' nose, then she turned, walking to leave out the bedroom. Macho's eyes fell down her back to her phat jiggling ass. His dick grew as hard as a steel pipe at the sight of it. He wanted so badly to put his face between them and make G-Baby's toes curl while she moaned his name.

Dreams barked at him just then.

"Shut cho' ass up," he told her, then got out of bed, now that his dick wasn't throbbing like a beating heart anymore.

G-Baby

"Why, why, whyyyy? Why did I go in there and ask him to work out with me? Goddamn, that nigga is fine! Fuck!

G-Baby had done the best that she could to not look at Macho's chiseled upper body, but his body was like a big muscular magnet that refused to let her eyes go. He was like a big piece of vanilla red velvet cake that she wanted to taste and savor, prolonging the delicious end for as long as she could.

Heading down the stairs, she made her way to the basement, where Macho and Yessy had their own state-of-the-art exercise area / weight room. And with every step she took, she grew even more nervous and excited about seeing him hot, sweaty, muscles bulging, and breathing hard like he had just pounded some pussy like the wild animal in bed she was yearning to see about for herself.

Macho

He threw on a tank top and his work-out Jordans, brushed his teeth, then headed down to the kitchen with the dogs. After he got them fresh food and water, he went to the pantry and got more feeder fish for his caimans.

As soon as the fish hit the murky waters of their lagoon, the mini gators snapped them up as if it'd been days since they'd eaten. Macho watched them devour the fish, then they all turned their heads to look at him.

"I can't wait 'til y'all get a little bigger. I'm puttin' y'all to work," he told them, then made his way to join the Gangsta Boo.

***

Reaching the weight room / gym, Macho heard the sound of Future's "Birds Take a Bath," featuring Young Jeezy and Young Scooter playing. He rounded the corner to the spacious area and foam nearly swallowed his breath when he saw forty-three-inches of Puerto Rican booty up in the air.

G-Baby was bent all the way over, stretching out her hamstrings. She heard him approach and stood upright. She turned around and saw the look on his face. Unable to help it, she started laughing.

"You good?" she asked, knowing that look anywhere.

"Uh…yup ...I'm Gucci," Macho capped, mentally willing his dick to not get hard.

"Okay. Let's do it," G-Baby said then.

Maaan…this girl is poison…sexy poison…with a big phat ass booty.

After they stretched, they did a quick cardio warm-up of Burpees, with two pushups, doing ten reps. They did ten sets, then went onto the weights when their blood was nice and hot.

They began with bench pressing. G-Baby lifted the hundred-pound barbell, while Macho repped two twenty-five like it was seventy-five pounds. They turned up after five sets and increased their reps by ten. Once they'd completed ten sets of twenties, they moved onto doing shoulders. They did shoulder-presses with light weights but lots of reps. Leaving arms for another day, they finished with H.I.I.T- High Intensity Interval Training, which was hyper-fast cardio. By the time they were finished, they were drenched in sweat, hearts beating a mile a minute in their chests, breathing hard to catch some air in their lungs.

G-Baby looked at Macho. His massive form bulged like his muscles knew no boundaries of size. Her nipples got so hard that she felt the need to put on a shirt so he wouldn't see them through her sports bra.

Macho felt eyes on him. He looked at her and caught her staring.

"What?" he asked.

"Huh?" she replied, furrowing her eyebrows at him.

"You starin' at me like you wanna box," he told her.

She twisted her lips up. "Maaaan, I'll beat cha' ass, Macho," she said, waving him off.

Macho slid right up to her faster than she even thought him capable of, from being so damn big.

"I don't think I heard you." He leaned down and put his forehead to hers, looking her in her eyes. "Care to repeat that?"

G-Baby looked up into his eyes and had to use all her mental strength to keep herself from rising up on her tippy toes and stealing a kiss. She managed to curl her lips into a smirk, while standing her ground.

"I said, I will beat chu' the fuck up, yellow-ass nigga. Now get cho' ass up outta my face before I eat cho' nose," G-Baby said, not moving an inch, despite how moist her panties were and not from sweating.

Macho stepped back, throwing his hands up in playful surrender.

"You got it, Miss Gangsta Boo. I don't want no 'shmoke wit' Vanessa Rojas, yo."

"Who the fuck is that?" G-Baby asked, puzzled by the name.

Macho chuckled as he compared G-Baby to the brown-skinned Latina detective on the show *Chicago P.D.* He was about to tell her when his phone started ringing. Leaving her with a scowl on her face, Macho went and got his phone from off the table.

"Eeeeee, my lady lieutenant calls upon her street king," Macho said, then answered the call. "Pero que pasa bonita, soldier girl?"

He put it on speaker phone so G-Baby could hear, as Yessy chuckled at him.

"You sound all hyped up 'n shit, yo. Why you so happy? Gabi must be makin' breakfast."

"Naw, we workin' out, we just finished up with that H.I.I.T shit. Yo, that shit ain't no joke, bae."

Macho and G-Baby heard Yessy laugh.

"It most definitely ain't. Imagine if you'd have been in the military with Gabi and me, all the PT we had to do and hear all them cocky-ass niggaz talk shit about us 'cause we females."

"I woulda' got kicked out, 'cause I would've beat all they ass for doggin' my lady and my G."

Off to the side, G-Baby busted out laughing. She laughed so hard that she fell to the floor.

"Why is she laughing like that?" Yessy asked.

Macho looked at G-Baby. "Yo no se. What time you gettin' off?"

"None of ya' bizness. See ya when I get there. Love you!"

Yessy ended the call before he could say it back to her.

Macho shook his head, chuckling to himself. He turned and saw G-Baby still on the floor, just lying there. He went over to her and looked down at her. "Plannin' on takin' a nap or somethin', Gangsta Boo?"

She looked up at him and twisted her lips at him.

Macho reached down and took her hand, helping her up. For a minute they both just stood there, staring into each other's eyes. Then Macho spoke. "You gon' make me flip yo' lil ass if you keep starin' at me like that."

"Nigga, you ain't gon' do shit," G-Baby challenged.

Macho went to grab her, but G-Baby saw it coming.

She dropped down and propelled herself through his legs, then popped back up. By the time Macho had gotten turned around, G-Baby was in the air and a second after, he was on the floor, with her on top of him, pinning his wrists down above his head.

"What the hell?" he said, bewildered at what had just happened.

"You might have forgotten, but I'm from Chicago and I was in the military. I'm not easy to beat, half-breed."

Macho wasn't thinking about how he had ended up on his back. He was thinking about how he could so easily flip her off him, get her onto her back, pull her leggings down and nail her thick ass to the cross.

G-Baby

She gasped and immediately jumped up off him when she felt his hardness under her. Macho stayed where he was, unable to move. She reached her hand down to him. It took him a minute to accept the help.

"Uh…you tryna' ride with me to Eve's crib? She said she needs to holla at me," Macho said, relieved that once again his hard dick had softened before G-Baby could see what she did to his libido.

G-Baby nodded. "Sure. We can get somethin' to eat first."

"Yeah."

She smiled at him. Turning away, she hurried off to get away from him, before the heat he radiated turned her into a puddle on the floor.

Macho

Maaaan, that ass is PHAT! *Daayuum*! Macho thought, watching G-Baby hurry towards the stairs. He took a deep breath to calm himself, then he grabbed his phone, and headed to the stairs to get upstairs and get showered and fresh.

***

Forty-odd minutes later, Macho was fresh and clean in a distressed denim jean and jacket Balenciaga fit, with wheat Timbs on his feet, his white-gold and diamond Cuban link chain around his neck, diamond studs in his ears, his white-gold Richard Mille on his wrist, and a diamond pinkie ring on. Rubbing on a little Versace cologne, he left out of the bedroom to meet up with G-Baby.

Maaaaan, come on, yo! *Why*? *What the fuck she gotta be lookin' all good like that for*? Macho thought when he saw her coming down the stairs.

G-Baby was dressed in a tight, shoulder-less, all blue mini-Gucci dress, with Gucci monogrammed all over it. With the form-fitting thigh-high ensemble, she wore blue pantyhose that also had Gucci signs monogrammed in them. The white leather Gucci stiletto boots she had on went up to her knees. Her hair was loose, hanging down her bare shoulders. She wore a blue Gucci bucket hat, and white Gucci shades with blue lenses. Her lips were glossy blue and hanging from her ears and neck were white gold diamond drip. The diamond encrusted Rolex on her wrist sparkled, as did the diamond rings on her fingers, and the diamond tennis bracelet she wore opposite the Rolie.

"Well damn, shortie, we ain't goin' to the BET Awards," Macho said, as her high-heeled boots touched the main level floor.

G-Baby looked at him incredulously. "I know you ain't talkin'. Man, bring yo' ass on, Macho. I'm hungry as fuck, Joe."

I got somethin' you can eat on, Macho thought, as he followed behind G-Baby's phat round ass, dick swelling up in his Tom Ford boxer briefs so much that he swore he might bust a nut if he looked at it for another five seconds.

Chapter 16

Yessinia

"Major Morales," said Colonel Pane, looking at her. "I'm honored to have had such a warrior in my squad. I'm sad to see you go, but I find joy in knowing that you and our recently discharged Captain Medina are on to bigger and better things. I hope you two will never forget us poor ol' Army folk."

Yessy chuckled. "I could never do that, sir. You are all my family. It was an honor to serve with you and kick a little ass while doing it."

Colonel Pane nodded his head. "I've been mulling over what you and Captain Medina had been requesting. Are you two still interested in obtaining a civilian Department of Defense contract?"

Her eyes lit up with excitement. "Yes, sir, we are."

"Your reputations precede you both, and your records were impeccable. I really like the fact that you both are teaming up together. I feel that you two will do a great job and possibly blow all the other civilian contractors out of the water. Your team of ex-military personnel also is a plus in my eyes. I will make a call, and you have my word, I will be getting back to you very soon."

Again, Yessy did all that she could to contain her excitement, but hearing that her colonel, who most definitely had the power and connections to make it happen, was going to help her and G-Baby out, had her ready to jump for joy.

"I'd like to ask a question, though, Major Morales, if I may?" Colonel Pane said.

"Yes, sir, I'm all ears," Yessy replied, making eye contact with the massive African American war veteran.

"I've heard many times that you're in a relationship with a known cocaine trafficker. If this is true, then I may have a problem with the higher powers that I'll have to tap on to get this done."

Yessy didn't falter a tiny bit. She showed no fear, nor apprehension.

"Colonel Pane, sir, with all due respect, my boyfriend is a good man. He is one of the most selfless men on this planet. All he does for people…he does it without expecting anything in return. His mother and father, may they rest in peace, raised him the right way. He is a truck driver and only hauls high-dollar freight." In no way did she lie, but she never said what her man hauled in specifics.

Colonel Pane nodded his head. "Alright, Major. I'll give you a holler when I know something. For now, I think there's a surprise waiting for you in the mess hall."

"A surprise?" Yessy questioned, as her colonel came around his desk.

"Yes, Major. You didn't expect for us to let you discharge without a hell of a last day on base, did you?"

Yessy smiled. "I'm gonna miss wearin' this sir," she said, looking at herself garbed in her fatigues and combat boots.

"You kicked a lot of ass in that uniform, Major. Don't worry, though, I'm sure there'll be some ass to kick wherever you end up! Now let's go see everyone that wants to spend some time with you before you become a civilian again."

Yessy nodded her head. "Yes, sir."

G-Baby

She nodded her head to Curren$y's "In The Sun," featuring French Montana as it bumped from the subwoofers in the trunk of Macho's Mulsanne. Riding shotgun, G-Baby was leaned back in her seat, relaxing and trying to keep her mind off of Macho. The way he gangster leaned while he whipped the big Bentley was even sexy to her.

Why? Why can't I stop wanting him? He is my friend! It's not supposed to be like this, man! She thought, feeling so very ashamed of lusting over her best friend's man.

Macho

Fuuuuck, goddammit…goddammit…goddammit! She smells so good! he thought, as her candy-scented perfume made his mouth water.

Glances to his right landed on her thighs. The hem of her tiny dress had ridden up so far that her goodie box wasn't far from being visible.

He did all he could to focus on the road as he headed east down Route 173. Ahead, the intersection for 173 and Kenosha Road was coming up. The light turned red before he got to it.

Future's "Itchin" came on as he came to a stop. It cut off when a call came through. Macho saw Javi was calling. "Yo?" he answered.

"Nigga, tell me you around!" urged Javi.

Immediately, Macho could hear anger in his cousin's voice. G-Baby sat upright in her seat, alerted to the urgency.

"I'm in the Z. What happened?" Macho asked.

"Come to the Village, cuz! ASAP!"

The call ended with nothing more said. Macho mashed the gas and whipped his car to the right onto Kenosha Road. Ten seconds ahead of him, the entrance to Zion's big Horizon Village apartment complex was on the right. He whipped it into the entrance and flew down the main drive, already knowing exactly where his cousin had called him to.

Javi

"Come on, bro, please! I didn't know, man! I swear to God!" cried Teddy, one of Zion's well-known coke boys. He sold a lot of crack and a lot of powder, but recently, his product had been discovered to be tainted with a bad cut. Yet, he continued to sell it. Now, he regretted it. "Nobody told me the shit was killin' people! You gotta believe me! Money don't come from dead people, Joe!"

Javi listened to the man, but couldn't care less about what he was saying, and neither could his wife.

Tied to a chair in the middle of his living room, Teddy was terrified. He knew who the green-eyed Dominican was, and what it meant that he was there.

Michelle came out of the kitchen a second later. Sha had a turkey baster in her hand, filled with liquid. Teddy looked at her, as she went back to her husband's side.

"Please, man! Say somethin', Joe! This silence is killin' me!"

Javi chuckled. "You think that's killin' you? Oooweee! In about…" He looked at his Ferrari Hublot from the time. "…thirty seconds, the silence is the last thing that will be killin' you."

Teddy looked back and forth at the man, then the woman. They both stood there, staring at him, not even blinking.

Just then, the glass patio doors slid open. Javi and Michelle looked up and saw Macho enter, with G-Baby right behind him.

Javi nudged his wife's side with his elbow.

"If you say it, I'll smack the fuck out cho' ass, Javier," she threatened, already knowing what he was going to say.

"Sup, cuz. This is Theodore, aka Teddy Bitch," Javi said to Macho. "Found out he is at least one of the clowns movin' that hot shit out here."

Macho and G-Baby stopped in front of Teddy. He looked up at Macho and pissed his pants. As much as he knew who Javi was, he was even more afraid of El Tiguere. Macho's name rang big Notre Dame bells around.

"Whaz hanin', Teddy? Where you get the yayo from?" Macho asked him.

"P-P-Please, bro! I c-can't snitch!"

CRACK!

G-Baby rocked his jaw hard.

"You might wanna' reconsider, my nigga," Macho warned him. "She will fuck you up."

"I got it from a Mexican!" Teddy said then.

CRACK!

G-Baby socked him again, this time in his right eye.

"Bitch ass nigga, do you not know how many Mexicans are in the Midwest? Let alone Illinois!" she snapped.

"He's from Milwaukee, man! I met him at the Wal-Mart on 173! I paid for a brick and that was all!"

CRACK!

She splowwed Teddy again.

Macho looked at her. "Why you hit him again? He just gave us some information."

"Cause his bitch ass just snitched!" G-Baby spat venomously.

Javi, Michelle, and Macho busted out laughing.

"Ta loca, esta tipa," Macho said of G-Baby. "Aye, Teddy, I can save you a broken jaw if you call dude and tell him you need more."

Teddy gasped. "But I just—"

CRACK!

G-Baby fired on his ass again.

"You should only be sayin', 'Okay! I'll call him!'" G-Baby said.

"Okay! I'll call him!"

"Good job, bitch ass nigga. Where's yo phone?" asked Macho.

G-Baby

"Nigga, ain't no way yo' ass ready for more yet! You ain't dumpin' like that! Yo' ass po-lice! Fuck off my line!"

The call ended. G-baby lowered the phone and looked at Macho.

"See! I told you!" Teddy said.

SMACK!

Michelle's open hand smacked the shit out of Teddy.

"Goddammit! That shit hurt!"

WHAM!

Javi rocked Teddy's jaw, making him yelp in pain.

"Shut up, bitch!" he shouted.

Macho took the phone from G-Baby and sent the number to Teddy's supplier to ChaCha, telling her to get it tracked. A thumbs-up emoji came second after Macho sent it.

"Well. That concluded this meeting," he said, looking at Michell and her turkey baster. "Care to do the honors, cuzzo?"

"With pleasure."

G-Baby grabbed Teddy's head and held it against his will. Macho and Javi watched Michelle stick the nozzle of the baster into Teddy's left nostril. He bucked and kicked but couldn't move.

Michelle pushed the plunger. A watered-down cocaine mix flew up his nose. Right away, Teddy's eyes went wide. He started convulsing, then soon, he began foaming at the mouth.

They all watched his eyes roll to the back of his head.

"What the fuck did you shoot up his nose?" G-Baby asked.

"Sheit, I don't know. It came from the coke he had in his bedroom. All I did was put a little water in it and filled the baster with it," Michelle told her.

"ChaCha has a sample. We'll find out what's in it soon," Javi said, as Teddy's heart exploded in his chest, and he went completely limp.

"Good. Can we go eat now?" G-Baby asked.

"Y'all tryna' ride wit' us? We finna go to the bro's spot on Sheridan," Macho said to Javi and Michelle.

"Naw. We gotta go meet up with her newest buyer. Bae got a fake-ass DJ Khaled ready to drop a buck on a couple of Cuban links she flossed," Javi said. "We'll meet up with you at ChaCha's, though. She wants us at her crib tonight at ten."

Macho nodded. "Bet."

"Y'all two go ahead," Michelle said. "We'll clean up in here."

"Aight. One, yo," Macho said, dapping his cousin up.

"Love, cuz," Javi replied.

Chapter 17

Macho turned into the parking lot of his brother's restaurant La Cocina de Capotillo, a spot that served up authentic Dominican cuisine. The lot was nearly filled for the lunchtime rush. He parked in the spot next to his brother's private slot and got out, opening the door for G-Baby. Like a gentleman, he took her hand and helped her out, then held the door for her as they entered the packed spot.

Right away, the Dominican waitresses that were busy serving hungry customers saw Macho enter and abandoned their sections, eager to tend to their boss' little brother.

G-Baby smacked her lips as the four hour-glass shaped Afro-Latinas tried to be the one to serve Macho. Laughing, Macho took G-Baby's hand and pulled her along as he chose to sit in Corina's section, which pissed Latia, Raven, and Paz off.

***

Orders of Frituras de Ñame—fried yam cakes—were brought out as appetizers until their meal came out, along with a couple tropical smoothies. Soothing Merengue music played, and with the Caribbean themed painting and color schemes, Tool's restaurant was like leaving Zion, Illinois, and stepping into Santo Domingo with no worries about anything but what you wanted to eat and drink.

***

Macho sipped his raspberry-blueberry cream smoothie, while lost in his thoughts. He was still thinking about the run-in with Roxanne. He didn't think he would see her again after he embarrassed her. The last thing he had heard about her was that she had been seen with a big baby bump, while playing desk jockey.

He was anxious to find out who was putting poison in the coke that very likely came from him. His brother was the underboss, second-in-power below Danny, and he himself was the enforcer. His job was to keep order, and when shit started going to the left, it was he who got it back on track.

***

"Macho?"

He looked up at G-Baby when she called him.

"Why yo' forehead all wrinkled up? What's on y' mind?"

"Too much. I'm ready to find out who's shakin' my yayo up and killin' people."

G-Baby nodded. "Me, too. That shit is wild. We really do need to find out ASAP. That shit has that bitch in blood hound mode."

Macho chuckled. "Right?"

His phone started ringing. Pulling it out, he saw Narco was calling.

"Dimelo," Macho answered.

"Can you talk?" Narco asked.

"Yup. What hanin'?"

"Trip's gettin' moved up sooner. Just got into it with my dad, so I need to hurry up and get it all up here, bro."

"Which is needed by when?"

"Two days max."

"That's a major push-up, yo."

"I'll pay you in advance, my nigga," Narco swore, sounding desperate.

Macho felt G-Baby's eyes on him. He looked up and saw her slanted eyes were narrowed at him.

"Aight. Say when and I'll ride."

"Yup."

He ended the call and saw G-Baby was still glaring at him.

"Yessy's gonna' fuck you up, Antonio."

"I cannot agree nor disagree with you, as I have no clue as to why you think this."

She raised an eyebrow up at him. "Uh-huh. You can play if you want to. She will find out, even if I don't tell her."

He opened his mouth to challenge her, but before he could, Corina arrived with their food.

"Bambas de camarones y papas fritas," she said, setting the plate of cylindrical-shaped cakes made of chopped shrimp and mashed potatoes, flavored with cheese, onions, and lightly dusted with egg and breadcrumbs. "Y para ella," Corina said and sat down G-Baby's plate of marinated fried chicken pieces with fried plantains. "Chicharrones de pollo, con platano frito."

"Macho, Macho! Toma, papa! Para ti," came Raven, with a big slice of Pastelon, similar to lasagna.

"Macho! For you, guapo!" said Latia, right behind her with a bowl of Cuipes, balls of seasoned meat that were like a snack.

"Surullitos, Macho!" came Paz, with a Puerto Rican plate of corn sticks with cheese in them.

"Well, damn! Thank you, mujeres. Muchisima gracias!" he repeated in Spanish.

"Seguro papi," purred Corina with flirty eyes.

"Vete pa carajo! Ahora!" G-Baby snapped angrily, smacking the table with her hand.

The people in the restaurant immediately stopped what they were doing, startled by the outburst. Corina and the others scattered, not wanting any trouble with the Gangsta Boo. They had heard a lot about her.

"Well, that was uncalled for," Macho said to her.

"And?" She scowled at him.

"And this food looks grrrreat! Want a suru—?"

"No!" G-Baby snapped, cutting him off.

"Okay, then…someone needs a nap," Macho muttered, then dug into his food, wondering why the Gangsta Boo had just blown her top like that.

***

"Goddamn, that shit was fire, yo!" Macho rubbed his stomach, feeling so full, he could fall asleep right where he was.

"Hell yeah," G-Baby agreed, sipping her melted papaya smoothie.

"Well, well, well. Lookie at who we have here."

No way…ain't no way this bitch is here…please lemme' be tweakin', he thought, hearing her voice but praying he was hearing things.

By the look in G-Baby's eyes as she looked beyond where he sat, Macho was sure that she was behind him.

A pair of little hands suddenly covered his eyes.

"Guess who, Macho," he heard her say.

"Nayeli…get off me, yo."

G-Baby

She was frozen in place but not with fear. She saw the bitch, the younger sister of the biggest snake in the world, in her eyes. G-Baby's blood started boiling when she laid eyes on the Aztec-brown-skinned Mexican chick.

The girl stood five-three but was taller in the pricey designer heels she had on. She looked like a model, in the brilliant fire engine red leather dress, with alligator accents, dripping with yellow gold and diamond jewelry. Her makeup looked professionally done, as if she was on her way to a beauty pageant. Her long brown hair was streaked with gold highlights.

Nayeli Florez was an amazingly gorgeous twenty-five-year-old woman, and G-Baby loathed her. Not only because she was Narco's sister, but because during a brief split between Yessy and Macho…Nayeli had been his jump off.

Absent-mindedly, G-Baby gripped her fork and pictured herself jabbing it into Nayeli's carotid and letting the bitch bleed to death. She saw there were four guys accompanying the girl, all of them in suits, looking like *Men In Black*. The second she saw Nayeli's hands touch Macho, G-Baby exploded.

Macho

"Nayeli! Get the—"

"Agghh!"

CRACK!

"Hey!"

Macho's eyes were uncovered the second he heard a loud crack, then a loud thung, and along with a man shouting, Macho heard a bunch of people gasping.

He turned around and saw guys in suits, rushing G-Baby to get her off Nayeli.

Macho saw red the second one of the large men grabbed G-Baby and snatched her clean off her feet.

G-Baby

"Hijueputa!" she heard Macho shout, then the man who had her hemmed up let out a loud yelp, then released her.

She fell to the floor on her ass, gasping for air. Filling her lungs back up, G-Baby saw Macho firing on the guy that had snatched her off Nayeli, who was still laid on the floor, bleeding from her nose and her busted lower lip.

Two of Nayeli's guards ran up and grabbed Macho. People in the restaurant were all spectating, filming with their smartphones. She even saw thirsty-ass waitresses, all looking scared, off the side.

"Get the fuck off of me!"

The sound of Macho's yelling brought G-Baby back. She saw the two guys muscling him away from their bloody co-worker, slamming him on the floor, while the fourth helped Nayeli up.

"Oh, hell no!" G-baby said, and jumped up to go help her homeboy out.

Right before she could get to them, G-Baby caught a glimpse of a flash, then heard a loud crack. One of the guards flew sideways, hit the floor hard, and didn't get up.

She then saw Yessy's six-foot-two-inch-tall, caramel-skinned younger brother go at the second guy, putting his MMA training into overdrive and going berserk.

G-Baby then heard Nayeli screaming. She looked and saw her fatigued-clad best friend, gripping the Mexican belle by her hair and yanking her up by it.

Yessinia

"Puta! Te dije que si' alguna vez te veo cerca de mi fucking hombre, I would kill you!" she screamed, then slammed Nayeli's face down hard on the table.

Nayeli screamed in pain when her face was smashed into one of Macho's spicy plates of food. The spices got in her eyes, burning them so badly that she couldn't open them.

Yessy grabbed Nayeli and lifter her clean up over her head like a straight beast, then she hurled the girl at the wall. Nayeli cried out in pain as the wind was knocked out of her.

Macho

"Goddamn! My baby a G, yo! Homiez!" Macho exclaimed after seeing his Bad 'Rican toss Nayeli like she was a diva wrestler.

CRACK! CRACK! WHAM!

He spun around and saw Romeo still thumping. He had whooped the two that had taken him to the ground and was now on the one he had already bloodied up.

The twenty-two-year-old was Yessy's half-brother, they had the same Puerto Rican mother, but Romeo's father was African American. Yessy loved to say that Romeo was like the rapper N.O.R.E., but with long hair that was currently braided in single plait braids, hanging down his shoulders.

He was a young beast, nice with his hands, and the pistol play was his favorite. Most importantly, Romeo was a rider, especially for his sister. When it came to Yessy, Romeo would kill for her, and he would also die for her and vice versa.

***

"Rome! Lil bro!" Macho rushed to grab Romeo before he killed the guy with his bare hands. "Yo, come on, kid, relax. He's done for, lil' cutty."

Yessy rushed over with G-Baby as Romeo came up out of his frenzied state. Macho saw the young gunner's eyes turn back on.

"Yo, son, you good?" he asked Macho, with a raspy voice, so similar to the rapper NAS.

"Yeah, bro. I'm good. We should slide though. I guarantee Five-O is on the way," Macho said then.

They all made way to get to the exit. Before they got there, Macho heard G-Baby call out to them.

"Be right there! I gotta use the restroom!"

"Come on, Gabi, we gotta go!" Yessy urged, but G-Baby had already run off towards the ladies room.

Nayeli

"Fucking bitch! Bro, you need to send your goons down here right now!" she screamed, looking at her swollen and bloody face, in the bathroom mirror.

Her phone, the screen cracked, laid on the sink top, was on speaker mode, with the call time rolling.

"No," Narco said.

"What? What the fuck you mean 'no,' Narco? I'm your sister, motherfucker!"

"And you a shit-starter, I bet my crown that you started it, and you know how Macho's girls get down. Stop bein' a brat, Nayeli! We got plans! We need th—"

CLICK!

She ended the call on him.

"Bitch ass nigga! Fuck you, fat piece of caca!"

The bathroom door opened up just then. Nayeli saw G-Baby enter, with a smirk on her face.

"No! Hell no! Get out, bitch!" she demanded.

She took off her right high-heel and held it up with the heel pointed at G-Baby.

Nayeli saw the Boricua start walking towards her.

"Get back, bitch! I swear to God I'll stick this heel in yo' eye!"

G-Baby continued coming, her smirk growing even more sadistic by the step.

Nayeli shrieked when G-Baby got to within two feet of her. She swung the heel as hard as she could at G-Baby's face. G-Baby leaned back, avoiding the attempt. Nayeli swung again. G-Baby side-stepped it, then countered with a hard right jab.

Nayeli's head snapped to her right and before she could revoke, she was lifted off her feet when G-Baby's fist hit her under her chin.

She flew backwards to the nasty floor, immediately snatched back up.

"Since yo' thot-ass thinks you're the shit, I'ma put you where you belong!" G-Bay growled through clenched teeth.

G-Baby

"Ooowwww! Stoooop! Pleeeease!" Nayeli screamed, as G-Baby dragged her by her hair into the stall with the shitter in it.

Ignoring Nayeli's pleas and struggling, G-Baby muscled the petite Chicana's head into the toilet, filled with pissy water. Nayeli kicked and tried to pull herself out, but G-Baby was strong.

WHAM!

G-Baby punched her in the side, which made Nayli draw in a lungful of piss water. She let go seconds later and watched Nayeli flop onto the floor like a fish out of water. She cried her eyes out, as G-Baby smirked sadistically.

"If you ever contact Macho again, I will tie you up and put yo' ass on train tracks and watch you get smashed," G-Baby threatened.

She turned on her heels to go.

"Vete al infierno, puta!" She heard Nayeli scream.

G-Baby turned back around. Nayleli shrieked and tried to hide on the side of the toilet.

Laughing, G-Baby made her way out of the bathroom. She pushed the door open and almost ran into Macho.

She gasped in shock, then got lost in his bedroom blues.

"Sounds like you had a little bit of a struggle in there," he said, looking right into her eyes.

"Um…no more than usual."

Macho shook his head. "Tell me you didn't kill the little bitch in my brother's restaurant, Gabi."

"I didn't. I just gave that thirsty ass bitch a drink."

He laughed. "Come on, lil' Gangsta Boo, Yessy and Rome are waitin'."

"The cops come?"

"Came and left. Now come on n' let's go."

Chapter 18

Yessinia

Standing in front of her G-Wagon, with her brother, Yessy watched her man come out of the restaurant with G-Baby, slung over his shoulder, ass up in the air.

Romeo busted out laughing. "Yooo, Macho's a funny nigga, sis! He got the Gangsta Boo on his shoulder like she a runaway pup!"

Yessy shook her head. Macho set G-Baby on her feet when he got to where they stood, then he slid up on his woman and kissed her breath away.

Yessy was left with a stupefied expression on her face that had Macho laughing his ass off.

"Ooooweee. Fucked yo' head all the way up!" he teased.

"Shut cho' ass up and take me home, yo! I'm tired and cranky and need you to put me to bed," Yessy said.

"Man…don't nobody wanna' hear all that, yo," Rome said.

"Then close ya' muhfuckin' ears then, nigga!" Yessy shouted back.

Romeo waved it off.

G-Baby laughed. Macho gave her the key fob to his Mulsanne, then hopped into the G-Wagon with his woman.

Yessy led the way to the house, turning into the subdivision close to twenty minutes later.

She turned onto their street and saw the rare customer Fendi monogram-painted 2017 Lamborghini Centenario

Roadster in their driveway, with the tall, Amazon owner posted next to it, rocking a tight leather Fendi monogrammed dress, knee-high stiletto boots, and her long jet-black hair hanging loosely. With her, was her miniature horse of a dog, Pablo, a brindle furred Presa Camario that had the distinctive looks of a giant Pit Bull with clipped ears.

Yessy turned into the driveway and parked at the garage. G-Baby nosed Macho's Bentley up behind it.

Macho

"She looks mad," he said, looking through the dark tint, at the Colombian Puerto Rican billionaire street chick. Her arctic blue eyes were extra frosty and cold. She looked like she was ready to murk a whole block.

"Well, she's in charge of your family's entire world, someone's buying yayo at large quantities, adding some shit to it, and popping it off on the streets. People are dying, and feds are snooping. Who gets the ultimate blame, Antonio?"

Agreeing with her, Macho opened the door and got out. The big hundred and twenty-pound dog bumbled right up to Macho, nearly half his height, while on all four legs. Macho patted Pablo down, happy to see ChaCha's personal bodyguard / killer and companion.

Straight out of the East Coast, born and raised in New York's Jackson Heights section of Queens, ChaCha was incomparable to any other woman. She was ridiculously rich, fearless, and always ready to fight and shoot, but more than that, she was a loyal, loving, and big-hearted woman that was like a mother, big sis, and big cuz to Macho, his brother, their younger cousins, and all of the ladies of the Valdez family. She was revered by them all, and she loved them all dearly as well.

The magnificently gorgeous Latina was an alluring, model-type chick. She stood six feet tall, with a body type that was more than petite, but less than voluptuous. Her butter-pecan brown- skin radiated, and the tattoos she had on her arms, chest, neck and legs added to the sex appeal she exuded effortlessly.

She was thirty-two years old and had been putting in work for the Valdez family since she was eighteen, when Deanny had recruited her. It was right after she destroyed one of his homies that thought she could be wooed out of the panties and got disrespectful with her when she laughed at him.

***

"I know that look," Macho said to ChaCha. "When I see it, a lot of people die."

ChaCha gave a slight chuckle. "Tenemos que hablar. Let's go inside, papito," she told him, right as Tool bent the block in his Range Rover.

They waited as he parked at the curb. He hopped out with a young female German Rottweiler pup that he named Angel, and his dark-chocolate Belizean girlfriend, Tamalita.

Excitedly, the ladies greeted the SCM boss, and his beautiful five-foot-five-inch-tall woman. Their pup ran up to Yessy, wagging her butt, remembering that Yessy's dog was her sire, and was eager to see Papa Maliante.

They all headed into the house, ang gathered in the big living room. Yessy got everyone's beverages, then took a seat on her man's lap. ChaCha stood in front of them, and with anger and frustration, she began to speak.

As her words came out, Macho, Tool, Yessy, G-Baby and Tamalita began boiling with anger. Romeo wasn't involved in the Valdez family biz, but on behalf of his sister, and how he saw Macho amd Tool as his big brothers, he was ready to jump in himself.

"So where do we start, Prima?" asked Macho, ready to get on it.

"Every fucking body that pushed coke in Zion, Waukegan, Nogo, Round Lake," ChaCha said, as her dog grunted and gave a deep bark, which prompted Maliante and his daughter to do the same, while Dreams licked her chops, ears perked up as she sensed that it was time to go to work.

"No me importa, carajo. If they push yayo, the gon get holla'd at until we find who it is that's buyin' up shit and puttin' fentanyl in the shit. I don't even care if it isn't our coke, yo. We on that wit' 'errybody, B." She looked at Macho then. "The number you had me look into…I sent your details in an encrypted email. Handle that, yo."

Macho immediately got his iPhone out and checked the e-mail. Yessy read along with him.

"Gabi?" Yessy called out to her.

"Yeah?"

"Might wanna get changed outta that expensive dress, ma. This gon' be a bloody one."

"Say less," G-Baby replied and hopped up to get changed.

Yessy leaned over and kissed her man's forehead, then she went to get changed as well.

Macho's phone rang a second after his women left. He saw Narco was calling. Knowing better than taking his call in front of his people. Macho got up and excused himself. Walking off, he could feel their eyes on him, even as he stepped into the adjoining kitchen.

"Yo, what up, cutty?" Macho answered.

"I'm "bout to pull up at yo' crib, bro. I need a one-on-one wit' chu' real quick," said Narco.

"No! Don't pull up! I'll meet you in the back, bro! Whatever you do, Narco, do not pull up at my crib!"

He ended the call, snuck out to the garage, and opened it up. Hopping on G-Baby's crotch-rocket, Macho started the engine, put the kickstand up, and kicking it into gear, he hurried out of the garage before anyone could question him.

G-Baby

She heard her motorcycle's engine start-up as she pulled on a pair of black leggings.

"The hell?" G-Baby said and ran to her window.

She saw Macho dip out of the garage on her bike and shoot up the street. Mixed with the sounds of her GSXR, G-Baby heard the unmistakable sound of a supercharged Hemi engine.

Opening her window, G-Baby looked up the street and saw the black and gold Dodge Challenger Hellcat racing up the entrance road, heading towards the rear of the subdivision. She then saw Macho cut left at the end of the street and get behind the Challenger.

"Son of a bitch…YESSY! SIIS!" she yelled out loud, knowing for a fact that the Nuyorican would step in without hesitation, to break up the secret meeting that G-Baby felt should not be about to take place.

Macho

At the rear corner of the subdivision, Macho leaned G-Baby's bike on its kickstand as he cut the engine off. He got off the bike and posted as the driver's door to the blacked-out Hellcat 2-door with twin gold racing stripes, raised up Lamborghini-door style. The engine cut off and out came a black leather Guiseppe Zanoti sneaker then a hairy leg with a tattoo of a pitchfork going down.

The rest of the hefty Aztec-brown Mexican got out of his car, rocking black Balmain jeans, with gold zippers, a black t-shirt with Balmain Paris, in gold letters across this chest.

His long hair was free of the braids he normally wore and was pulled back into a ponytail. On his head, a black Brewers snapback, custom-stitched in gold. He dripped with diamond studs in his ears, a yellow-gold and diamond Cuban link, fitted with a matching five-point crown charm around his neck. A yellow-gold Patek Philippe flossed in yellow diamonds was on his left wrist.

He was tatted like he lived in a tattoo shop. Sleeved up with a big Latin King master on his left forearm holding a pitchfork upside down, while sitting on a throne. On the left side of his neck, a lion wearing a crown, had the letters ALKN under them.

Narco had no intentions of ever hiding when he had pledged allegiance to, when he was a shorty. Growing up with gangsters and drug dealers was his world. His father was the boss of one of the biggest cartels to come out of Tijuana. The Flores Cartel had taken over, since the Rojas-Gomez Cartel was no more.

Macho had initially met Narco during a short stay at Kenosha County Detention Center, in Kenosha, Wisconsin. He'd been booked on criminal damage to property charges, after he allegedly blew up a Pleasant Prairie police car.

While he was in, Macho got the eyes of the sex-and-love deprived female C.O. that worked there and became the object of their lustful fantasies. Many of the other detainees grew extremely jealous of him, mostly due to the fact that they wanted to be able to bump C.O. chicks but couldn't. A lot of people knew who Macho was, and who he was related to. Some feared him, and some wanted to take him out. Plots were made against him to get him up out the way.

One day, Macho was inside the inner recreation area, doing a strenuous cardio workout, when seven men that he knew had issues with him entered, and pretended to work out as well. They didn't know Macho knew that they wanted smoke. Always being the type to stand on his own two feet, he was ready for whatever.

The time came minutes after they geeked themselves up enough to try him. Surrounding Macho, they started doing what most guys in jail or prison did…talking shit with no action.

Macho waited patiently for the first time one or two would run up and get done up. Just as all seven of them attempted to move in when they saw him just smirking at them, Narco and his crew of ten of his King brothers entered the work-out area and put the brakes on the ambush immediately. Narco was known all around Wisconsin, especially in his hometown. The men that were about to get Macho, were terrified of Narco. The second he gave them just a look, they tucked their tails and flew up out of the area faster than a convicted murderer that had been vindicated and freed.

After that day, Macho and Narco got cool. Narco knew who Macho was, but it wasn't until later down the line when Macho finally was granted bail by his judge that he found out who Narco was.

They ended up linking up on the outs and getting a little money together. Macho went above and beyond to help the man get product up from Mexico, supplied by his drug lord father's competition. Macho didn't see Narco as that. He saw him as a friend that was just trying to get his piece of the pie as well.

Yessy was livid. When she'd met Narco, he creeped her out. She couldn't put her finger on what it was, but something in his eyes made her feel like she was looking in those of a python.

A year had gone by, and business between Macho and Narco had been fruitful. Narco celebrated surpassing a milestone in his newfound wealth, by throwing a party in his hood. He invited Macho to join him. Despite pleas from Yessy and G-Baby and ChaCha, Macho went and ended up almost catching lead when a rival gang called the Mexican Posse, a clique of Sureños 13 that had been notoriously beefing with the Latin Kings, had pulled up and sprayed at the party.

People on both sides had gotten hit, and many didn't survive. A group of MPs caught Macho and cornered him with SKs. He had come within seconds of joining the dead, when Narco came dumping on them, catching them all.

***

The five-foot-ten-inch-tall Latin King dapped Macho up, embracing him in a brotherly manner.

"What's goodie, bro? You ought!" Macho asked, seeing frustration in Narco's eyes.

"Not even close, my nigga. Why you keep lettin' yo' ladies beat my sister up?"

"I didn't let anyone do anything, Nayeli got stuck at the mouth. You know how they get down."

Narco nodded. He indeed knew how Yessy and G-Baby did things.

"And what cha' mean, my ladies? I have one woman."

Narco twisted his lip up. "Uh huh! Tell me anything. But look, though. I came in person to tell you I got more beef on my hands now, bro. It's gon' get really ugly fast."

"Wit the MPs again?"

"Naw. With my dad, bro. HIs old ass scared to let me start pushin' product up north of Wisconsin and the northwest. His ass gon' tell me 'No, mijo, we can't move in on the Natives territories! It's disrespectful!'"

"Macho chuckled. "And what did you do after that?"

"I choked his ass and then I blew up that old-ass Bugatti he love so much."

His eyes went wide in shock. "You blew up that type 57?"

"Hell yeah! Fuck him!"

"Nigga, that car was worth more than thirty million! What the hell is wrong with you, Narco?"

"If he gon' treat me like he think I'm a peon, bye-bye Bugatti!"

Macho was appalled by Narco. His own father had cars that had multi-million-dollar price tags, as old as his grandfather. He knew if he ever damaged any of them, he was in deep shit.

"Bro, you buggin'. If he on some cut you off shit, then you could've just hit me up. You know I got 'caine by the truckload, bro. Homiez, and player prices."

"It ain't lookin' too good for yo' yayo right now though, my nigga. Somebody's doin' you real bad, spikin' yo' shit like that."

Macho shook his head. "I'll handle it. Believe that."

Just as Narco was about to speak, they both heard what sounded like a huge swarm of bees. They looked up and saw the source of the noise coming towards them…fast.

"Bro…" Narco squinted his eyes to focus in better at the object as it got closer and closer. "What the fuck is that thing?"

Macho shook his head and cursed under his breath. "A very expensive car repair bill, if you don't get that pretty little Hell kitty outta here, yo'," he said.

Squinting so that he could see the drone better, Narco then saw what looked like a machine gun nozzle under the bulky flyer. When he put two and two together, his eyes went wide.

"Oh shit! Man, are you serious right now?" he asked as he started stepping towards his car.

"Yes. My woman is crazy and very protective," he told Narco as the man hurried and jumped into the Hellcat.

Macho watched the drone come to a hover above Narco's car, wondering why the hell he was still there instead of hauling ass. Macho looked into the whip and saw Narco seemingly fidgeting around, as if he was looking for his keys. "Push-start, foo'!" he shouted to Narco, just as flames shot out of the drone's nozzles, hitting the roof of the car.

Narco panicked, ducking down as the roof of his car was fired up. Macho shouted for him to get the hell on before he got cooked all the way. Frantically, Narco hit the push-start and fired up the powerful supercharged Hemi engine. Slamming it into gear, he mashed the gas and made his rear wheels disappear in a thick cloud of smoke.

Macho watched as Narco fled. The drone flew after the Hellcat, chasing it until Narco was on Green Bay Road and high-tailing north.

"That girl is nuts, yo," Macho said to himself, shaking his head. He hopped back onto the GSXR and rode off heading home, where he just knew everyone was likely in tears from laughing so hard.

Chapter 19

Yessinia

She was dying laughing. G-Baby, Tool, ChaCha, and Tamalita were in tears from how hard Yessy had them rolling. Romeo had no actual clue as to why his sister had nearly torched the guy's car. The remote to the drone in her hands had a screen that provided real-time view feed, via the camera mounted to the drone. He had seen it all, and he too was laughing his ass off.

***

The sound of G-Baby's crotch-rocket got her attention. They all looked up towards the top of the block and saw Macho bending the corner. From the front porch, Yessy and the others watched him coast down the street and wing into the driveway. He stopped by the sidewalk path to the porch and looked at her.

"Really?" she heard him ask.

"What? I missed breakfast, so I was in the mood for some bacon, bae," Yessy joked.

They all busted out laughing. Macho shook his head and rolled into the garage, where Dreams, Maliante, and Pablo were laid out next to a big fan to get a little relief from the heat, with Angel laid up with her sire.

"Great. Now he's mad at me," Yessy said, as she skillfully landed her drone back on the roof.

"He'll get over it," said Tal.

"Him 'a learn one way or 'de 'otha'," said Tamalita, with an accent similar to a Jamaican.

Yessy gave the remote to her drone to G-Baby, then gave her homegirl a sly grin.

"Uh oh. Yo' ass on some bullshit, Joe," G-Baby said, chuckling at Yessy.

"Go on 'n get 'dat crazy boy," Tamalita said, rooting for Yessy. "Ya' kick his ass good, 'ya hear me 'gurl?"

"Tama, she is not about to beat him up," ChaCha informed her.

"Here we go again with that TMI shit, yo," Romeo commented.

"Soooo…we'll see you in a bit," Yessy said, walking off to go find her man and make him stop being mad at her, whether he did so willingly or by force.

She searched all over the house for him. The upper level, the first floor, the backyard. He was nowhere in sight. When she discovered that Fats wasn't in the lagoon with the other caiman, she knew exactly where he had gone.

Heading to the basement door, she opened it up and could hear the sound of Lil Wayne's "Pussy, Money, Weed" playing.

Smiling evilly to herself, Yessy stepped down onto the first step and closed the door behind her. Softly, she stepped all the way to the bottom. She peeked around the corner, and saw him, laying on one of the couches in the lounge section. He was on the phone, talking to someone.

She started ginning as she thought of something that would make him forget all about her attempting to fry Narco's car and concentrate on nothing but thick sexy caramel Nuyorican.

Macho

"No. She plays too much," he said, still irritated.

"Ay carino, tranquilo," his grandmother Carolina said. She was a woman wise beyond her sixty-nine years of life, of which she had endured hardships and wars, as the family's multi-billion-dollar empire was built. She was her oldest and youngest grandsons' best friend, a big part of their life. "Don't be mad at Yessinia for trying to keep your payasos away from you, papa."

Macho sucked his teeth. "Ain't you supposed to be on my side, lady?"

"Hmmmm…when you are upset with her, because her torching hijo de puta's car, then no. Your woman is a rider, and if she does not like someone that comes around you, she will not be afraid to put her foot down, carino."

"Grandmother, I will call you back. The evil pork chop that bends on me for burning up a cop car, yet does the same thing is coverin' my eyes, so I can't see her diabolical plots on me."

Carolina busted out laughing. "Tell my future granddaughter-in-law I said hello, and I will see you all soon. Te quiero mucho, Antonio."

"I love you, too, Granma."

"Whatcha' doin'?" he heard Yessy ask, when he ended the call.

"Wonderin' why Fats ain't don' his job and guardin' me from you," attempting to get up, but was pulled back down. "¿Qué quieres, fire bug?"

"What I want, Antonio, is for you to stop callin' that bitch ass chunk of lard your homie, but I know that ain't gon' happen 'til your bullheaded ass sees the real him for yourself."

"My woman's a genius," Macho replied sarcastically.

"Shut up, asswipe. Anyways, since you can't give me that, then how about this?"

The next thing he knew, Yessy had uncovered his eyes. Macho blinked a few times as the bright lights temporarily blinded him.

He heard her tell him to turn around. Macho groaned but did as she said. He flipped himself around and his jaw dropped.

Yessy stood a couple of feet away from him ass naked, looking as sweet as a piece of caramel candy. He bit his bottom lip as his eyes roamed the epitome of Puerto Rican perfection. His dick instantly grew hard in his jeans. Then he shook his head and laid back down.

"Nope. That shit is dead, shortie. Yo' ass ain't finna put that woo on me and think your actions are excused, punk-ass pork chop," he said, selecting a game app to play.

"Nigga, stop fuckin' playing with me, yo!" Yessy snapped, stomping her feet on the ground.

"Shhhhh! I'm tryna concentrate!" he replied, commencing a game of Angry Birds.

"Motherfucker!" he heard her growl.

Macho chuckled to himself, then stopped when she snatched his phone from him.

"Yessy!" he shouted, hopping up from the couch to face her. "Stop playin' so damn much, yo! The hell wrong wit' chu?"

"Entonces, dame lo que quiero and I'll leave you alone!" she shot back, taking a step to him.

"You're lyin'," he replied.

"Yes, I am, now give me what I want, Antonio."

"Nope. You're beat, punk," he said, backing away from her, as she started advancing on him with the look of a horny woman with an insatiable sex drive. "Yo' ass better not touch me, Yessy."

She laughed at him. "Or what? You gonna kiss me?"

"No! You on dick-punishment!" Macho said, then attempted to run off from her.

Yessy grabbed him and pushed him back against the wall.

"Fuck you think you are going, Mr. El Tiguere?"

"Away from you, punk."

"Naw, yo. Check it out, my nigga. This what's gon' happen."

Yessy clapped her hands and activated the built-in audio system. Rick Ross's "You The Boss," featuring Nicki Minaj came on. "I'm bout to suck the shit out of your dick, then you gonna' beat this pussy up like you tryin' catch a charge. We gon' go shower after that, and then we gon go handle these clownz that wanna fuck wit' your family's legacy. Any questions?"

Macho couldn't help but to smile at his audacious Nuyorican goddess. She was truly a thoroughbred regulator. He loved how she was a take-charge-type woman, with such brains and beauty.

"Ma'am, yes, ma'am!" he said like a soldier to a sniper officer. "Permission to take yo' thick-ass to the couch, lay you down and eat that pussy up 'til yo' eyes roll to the back of ya' head and you call out my name as you explode in my face!"

Yessy chuckled. "Permission granted, Valdez. Get to it!"

He obeyed her, scooping her up off her feet, carrying her back to the couch, and sitting her down. With a smile that made her nipples grow hard, Macho leaned her back, opened her legs, exposing her. Then he kissed and licked from her lips down to her chest, breasts, stomach, arriving at her soaking wet box, ready to dive in headfirst like an Olympic swimmer that never wanted to leave the water.

Gabby

She groaned as her sexual frustration grew tenfold, envisioning it being her, getting it on with Macho. She closed her eyes and pictured it, while everyone else in the living room watched the red-head beauty on the show *Wild 'N Out* flame the fuck out of Conceded and DC Young Fly with her crafty bars.

ChaCha and Tool laughed their asses off.

"Yooooo, she be heatin' all they asses up! Agarra esos cabrones, Justina!" ChaCha shouted, cheering for who people sadly mistook as the underdog of the show, While Tamalita rooted for the white girl, alongside ChaCha.

Tool chuckled and took a sip of his cold Presidente beer. Romeo sat on another couch with Maliante by his feet. He was texting someone, not paying any attention to the TV show.

G-Baby gasped suddenly, making everyone's eyes fall upon her. She opened her eyes and saw six of them on her. Embarrassed, she jumped up and ran towards the bathroom, locking herself inside. She put her hand between her legs and felt how wet she was.

"What the fuuuuuuuuuuuuck, man!" she whined, tripping that she had actually just made herself climax in the seat while visualizing Macho pounding her out. "A bitch can't keep not a pair of panties dry whenever I'm within a mile of him! Que carajo!"

A knock on the door came just then. G-Baby hurried over to the sink and rinsed her hand. Then went to open the door. When she did, the piercing glare of arctic blue blue eyes nearly made her heart drop out of her ass.

"You okay?" asked ChaCha, with a raised eyebrow.

"Um…yeah…why wouldn't I be?" G-Baby asked.

She tried to step out, but ChaCha blocked her. She looked up at her and saw the look in ChaCha's eyes.

ChaCha stepped forward, ushering her back into the bathroom. She closed the door behind her, then stared down at G-Baby for a second. G-Baby felt her heart start to pound in her chest. Sweat formed on her forehead as she grew nervous beyond reason.

"Why are we in here?" she asked ChaCha.

"Because we need privacy, so that you can tell me exactly how long you've been in love with Antonio."

G-Baby's eyes went wide. She gasped at ChaCha's words.

"Bitch, don't even try it. You be all starry-eyed whenever you look at him, more now than before I really started noticing it. Then, you looked like someone stole your man when Yessy went to get hers. And let's not forget how you just left a puddle in the chair you was just mentally using to get off on, while you were likely thinking about Yessy and Antonio goin at it."

G-Baby was speechless. Her mouth opened up to respond, but she couldn't even begin to form worlds. ChaCha shook her head, not even needing to hear anything. She'd known for a long time that G-Baby was very attracted to Macho. Many people had known. Strangely enough, the only one that didn't seem to know…was Yessy.

"How long?" ChaCha asked again, folding her arms over her chest, not once taking her eyes off G-Baby.

G-Baby started tearing up then. She knew she couldn't lie to ChaCha. The woman knew so much that it was like she was a human brain. But how could she really admit that she was in love with Macho, to a woman who was like Macho's big sister, and who was like a big sister to Yessy, and to her as well.

"You know what?" said ChaCha, seeing how G-Baby seemed to be about to explode with emotional exasperation. "Don't answer, I already know. You'd do best to get yourself in check because I'm not the only one who sees it, though I am the only one who has spoken to you about it."

Tears began rolling down G-Baby's face as the dam threatened to break. ChaCha continued. "I honestly understand, mamita. He is a very gracious man, and although I know you aren't feeling the way you do because of how he made you rich, the way you care about him is normal. You are his best friend, and he is yours, but you need to keep that right there. You three have one of the strangest friendships I have ever seen before. Do not let lust ruin it, Gabriella. Me entiendes?"

G-Baby just nodded her head, unable to speak. She had just unspokenly admitted to the Valdez matriarch that she was in love with El Tiguere and now, she didn't know how ChaCha would look at her from that point on. It made her feel sick to her stomach. So sick that her stomach began churning.

She ran to the toilet and dropped to her knees, hurling her breakfast into the bowl. ChaCha shook her head, sighing to herself. She went over to the Gangsta Boo and held her hair out of the way while G-Baby puked her lusty guts up.

Yessinia

She cried out in bliss as she climaxed all over his lap. After three times in a row. Yessy felt fatigue setting in. Macho busted his nut right after she got hers.

Sweaty and worked out, Yessy laid on top of her naked Steel City Mafia goon, feeling so safe, warm, and loved. Her forehead rested on his. Her eyes were locked in with his.

"You still mad at me, baby?" she asked him.

"Yup."

She gasped, "What the fuck you mean, 'yup?' Don't be an asshole, yo!"

Macho laughed at her. Yessy reached a hand down and flicked one of his balls.

"Ow!" Macho jumped from under her, falling on the floor and cupping his nut sack. "Maaaan, what the hell is wrong with chu', Yessy?"

Now she was laughing at him.

"Shut cho' punk ass up!" Macho grabbed the pillow he had been laying out and clocked her with it.

"Aye!" Yessy grabbed the other and hit him with it.

"Fats! Get her!"

Yessy jumped, thinking the caiman was within biting range, until she discovered the mini alligator was at least ten feet away, resting under the bright lights.

Macho used the distraction and hit her with the pillow again.

"Motherfucker!" she screamed, pissed that she had just fell for it.

"Hey! Fats! Wake up and help a nigga out, lazy ass!"

Yessy took the opportunity and jumped on Macho, pinning him down on the ground.

"Haa! Now what, goddammit!"

Macho smirked up at her. "Piedras que ganaste, amore?" he asked.

Before she could give a reply, he bucked his hips, catching her off-guard enough to where he was able to flip her off of him and put her on her back, then pin her down with his own body.

Yessy tried like hell to buck him off of her, but she couldn't. He felt like a boulder on top of her.

"Goddammit, Antonio! This isn't fucking fair! You're heavy, yo!"

Macho started laughing at her, and then he pressed his lips to hers, and kissed her softly, passionately.

"Still unfair?" he asked, looking down into her eyes.

Yessy curled her lips up at him. "Yes!"

He kissed her again, this time, prying her lips apart with his tongue, and stocking it into her mouth. He pulled back after nearly a minute-long kiss.

"Y ahora?" he asked with a devilishly handsome smile that got her juices flowing again.

Yessy started pouting, trying so very hard to hold back her smile.

"Maybe," she capped.

He leaned in again, then kissed her to the point that Yessy felt like she might catch fire. Macho tongued his woman down for a few minutes, then pulled back. For another minute they gazed into each other's eyes, reading each other, their souls connected in ways that nobody could ever understand.

"Te amo, Antonio," she told him, as tears began filling her eyes.

Macho smiled at her. "I love you, too, Yessinia. You ready to go fuck some people up?"

Yessy giggled. "As long as we ride together, I'm always ready for whatever, mi amor."

Chapter 20

"Hold up, Joe. Fuck you comin' to me for, my nigga? You the one with the plug, Lil Five. Why are you here?" asked Mojo, a Sureño 13 fam out Round Lake.

"I don't got the plug no more, bruh, I gotta find another one. They asses got to taxin' me, plus I know you got the shit that's killin' it, Joe! On the Five, I needs that shit and I come wit' gwop. Tell me you finna pass up on thirty thousand like a dummy for two of 'em," the young light-skinned unknown Vice Lord with long, red-dyed dreadlocks said.

"You got thirty gees on you right now, Lord?" Mojo asked with devious eyes.

Lil Five lifted the hem to the bottom of his hoodie up to reveal three banded stacks of cash, ten grand each.

"When it comes to money, we don't fuck around, bruh."

Mojo smirked. "Well, come on in, Lord. I got two of 'em ready fa' ya' right now. On my crown, yo' custies gone' die to get they hands on more."

Lil Five stepped inside. Mojo went to close the door, but right before it closed…

BOOM!

The door was bashed so hard that it broke off the hinges. Mojo was hit by the door and flew forward to the ground.

"What the fuck, man?" he snapped.

Mojo flipped over and saw Lil Five now joined by a gorgeous woman, thick as hell with golden-blonde hair cut short on the right side of her head, and flawless golden-brown skin, holding a sledgehammer. With her, another thick-ass chick with auburn colored hair in twists and milk-chocolate skin.

"Knock-knock, Ese," the girl with the gold hair said. "Hope we ain't interruptin' nothin', but if we are, who gives a fuck!"

Mojo went to up the pistol he had tucked in his waistline. Lil Five ran up on him and kicked him hard in his face, breaking his nose instantly. He snatched the gun out of Mojo's waistline and cocked it, pointing it at his face.

Mojo sat up, nose gushing blood profusely. He looked at Lil' Five and the two ladies.

"Who the fuck are these bitches, Lil' Five, and do yo know how dead you all are, when my big homie finds out about this shit?"

Evelyn

Without any hesitation, the twenty-three-year-old Valdez family princess walked up with her sledgehammer and raised it up high over her head.

Mojo's eyes went wide with fear. He flipped over and tried to crawl away, but his attempts were futile. Evelyn brought the sledgehammer down hard, hitting him directly on his spine, instantly paralyzing him.

He cried when he realized what the girl had just done to him. Lil 'Five rolled him back over so Evelyn and her girlfriend could look into the man's eyes.

"Escuchame bien, mamahuevo," Evelyn said with narrowed eyes. "Who sold you that shit that you're selling to people, that's laced with fentanyl?"

Mojo looked up at her, terrified. She began raising her sledgehammer again up to do more damage, when he shouted out, "My big dog hit me wit' it!"

Evelyn lowered her hammer. "And what is his name?"

"They call him Mexico!"

"He stays out here?"

"Naw! He lives up in Milwaukee!"

Evelyn looked at her girlfriend. Gloria shook her head.

"Thank you, sir. Your honesty is appreciated," she then said.

Gloria reached into her hoodie's front pocket and pulled out a grenade. Mojo screamed in fear as she walked towards him with it.

BOC!

Lil' Five hit him in his left arm, blowing it off at the elbow. He blew his right arm off next. Mojo cried in agonizing pain, blood spewing out of the jagged stumps where his arms had just been.

Evelyn watched her girlfriend go and tuck the grenade in Mojo's pants. When she pulled the pin, they all ran out the house.

Right as they made it to the Range Rover that Evelyn bought him a couple years back, when she took Lil Five's former big Ghost homie's mob and made them her wolves, Mojo's house exploded.

Lil' Five mashed the gas and got them up out of there. Evelyn sent a text to her big cousin as they made a clean getaway, giving Macho the information she had gotten out of Mojo.

A thumbs up emoji was his response. Evelyn smiled to herself, then leaned back in her chair dying to hear what her brothers were going to do.

***

"Yeah, nigga. I'm on the way right now, fam! Chill out, Joe!" said Taz after yet another call about the two ounces and the half of powder his customer was blowing him up for.

"Hurry up, man! Niggas got clucks lined up down the block!"

"Nigga, I said I'm on the way!"

Taz ended the call. "Come on, bro. Let's go take care of this nigga and get this money so we can re-up."

His right-hand man, Low-Low, got up with the book bag of cash in his hand and two Glock 19s tucked in his waistline.

They left out of the house, hopped in to Taz's S550 Mercedes-Benz and left to dump the last of their laced yayo.

Half an hour later, after serving their customers, Taz hopped on the highway and headed north towards the Illinois-Wisconsin state line road. He got off of 94 at Russell, and went to the small Pilot truck stop at the end of Russell where it met Frontgate Road.

He saw his connect's blue '94 Cadillac Fleetwood on thirteen-inch Daytons laying on the ground via the hydraulics the 'Lac had.

Taz parked his Benz a few spaces away, got his Glock 21 from under his seat and tucked it, then grabbed the bag and got out.

***

The front passenger's door opened up as he approached. Taz got in with the long-haired Mexican and dapped him up.

"What 'oun, my nig?" Taz said, dapping the guy up.

"Shit. Gettin' this 'fetty, you dig?" replied Logo. "What chu' got for me, dog?"

BOOM!

"Oh, shit!" Taz shouted when the windows of Loco's Fleetwood shattered from an explosion so close to them.

"What the fuck, dog?" shouted Loco, in pain from shards of glass flying into his eyes.

Taz then saw his Benz was what had exploded. He gasped, realizing his homie had been inside, waiting for him.

He heard a whistle then. Looking forward through the windshield, he saw a man slightly taller than average, wearing a ski-mask. Long braids hung out from the bottom, reaching down to his chest.

Taz gasped when the guy pointed a Draco right at him.

"I can't see! Taz, I can't see, dog! What the fuck happened, my nigga?" Loco cried, reaching over and grabbing Taz, with blood leaking from both of his eyes.

"Karma," they both suddenly heard from Taz's blown open window.

Taz looked back to his right and saw a woman, wearing a ski-mask as well, holding a sawed-off shotgun.

"Taz! Who is that, man? Talk to me, dog!" Loco begged, damn near bout to shit his pants.

BOOM!

Loco felt a hot spray of liquid splash all over him after the loud blast of a shotgun.

"Taz!" He reached for the guy, only to discover what felt like a lifeless body. "Oh, shit! Taz! Aye, man!"

Loco jumped back against his door. It suddenly opened up, then he was grabbed and snatched out of his car.

"Help! Somebody help me!" he cried out blindly.

WHAM!

A blunt object crashed into his temple, knocking him right out, sending him to la-la land.

Macho

"Got a big ol' catfish on the line, cuzzo. We gon' eat real good tonight after I fillet this bitch."

Macho laughed at his cousin. "No doubt. Get back safely. We'll be done, here in a few, yo."

"Yo, cuidate, primo, " Javi said, and ended the call.

"Y'all ready?" he asked into the earpiece he was wearing.

"Been ready, papi," came Yessina's voice.

"Yep," came G-Baby's next.

"I'm ready, bro," Romeo checked in.

"Same here, papito," Macho heard ChaCha say a second later.

"Ready, lil bro," came Tool's voice.

"Alrighty then, people. Let's once again, show people how incredibly dumb it is to fuck wit' us," Macho said, then reached over and told Dreams that he'd be right back.

***

Corona stood up on a catwalk, high up over the main floor. Wearing a respirator, goggles, and a head cover, with a hazmat suit, he made sure he was fully protected from the dangerous fumes the kilos of fentanyl being mixed with the cocaine gave off.

On the main floor, fifty of his workers, all with the skills of chemists, cut brick after brick of cocaine. They had been at it for more than two weeks straight, getting minimal sleep, food and hardly had time to shower.

Corona had orders to get every ounce of the Dominican cocaine mixed with deadly proportions of the additive. The one he answered to was making it clear if anyone sought to buy product from the Valdez family, then they would pay for it with their life. And Corona was fine with it, as long as his money was on point.

"Lookin good down here, boss man," Corona said, speaking into his Bluetooth that was paired to his iPhone. "We should have it all cut up in a few more days, then I can send out word that the blanco that's putting people down comes from the Valdez family. Once people get too scared to buy from them, they'll be coming to you."

"That's the plan, dog. Make it happen," the boss said.

"Orale, Demonio," Corona replied, ending the call. He walked off, heading towards his office, where he had his own stash of cocaine that did not have the poison in it.

***

Inside, Corona got out of his hazmat gear, now looking like a suave GQ model in his Armani suit and shoes. He went to his desk, opened the top drawer, and pulled out the flat balsam wood carry case. He opened it up and smiled at the shiny powder inside.

Taking one of the bagged quarter ounces out, he ripped the package open, dumped it on his desk and got to crushing the pebble and boulders until it was ready to snort. He made huge Scarface lines and inhaled two of them, quick and fast, it hit him hard and fast. The euphoric bliss made his dick so hard that it felt like he was going to bust out of his trousers.

"Wooo!" Corona shouted, right after the sour backdrop oozed down his throat, numbing it with the rest of his body.

His breathing grew erratic. His heart pounded. He felt so alive, and horny.

Corona went to the phone that sat on his desk and dialed the number he had long ago memorized.

"Luscious Latinas? ¿En que te puedo ayudar?" the same woman answered, that always answered client calls.

"It's Corona, I want Ilinia ready for me right away. I'm gonna send a car for her."

"Claro que si, Senor Corona," the woman replied.

He set the phone back down, snorted another line, supercharging himself like an SRG-8 to a Hellcat.

He closed his eyes for a second, relishing the bliss of his favorite drug, then grabbed his iPhone to get a car to pick up his favorite escort.

KNOCK! KNOCK! KNOCK!

"Quien es?" Corona shouted.

"Soy yo, jefe! Domingo!"

"What do you want, cabrón? I'm busy!"

"We have to talk! There's a problem!"

Corona groaned and muttered a curse. He made his way to the door. Grabbing the knob, Corner heard what sounded like retching.

"Aye! You better not be puking at my damn door, pinche sucio!" Corona said, turning the knob. "What problem are we having?"

He opened the door then. He saw Domingo there, eyes wide, pupils dilated.

"Hey! Cabrón! Hablame!" Corona waved his hand in front of Domingo's face, but the man didn't move. "Domingo! Que chingao, guey?"

Suddenly, Domingo fell forward, hitting the floor face first. Corona gasped when he saw the ice pick sticking out from the back of Domingo's head.

"Dios Mio! Domingo!"

"Yo, my man."

Corona looked up when he heard the deep voice. The second he did, he locked eyes with a massively built man, with long braids, wearing all black, and a respirator. The look in his cold bluish eyes made Corona come close to catching the runs.

"Who…Who are you?" he asked, his heart pounding with fear.

"I'm the problem," the guy said, then he cocked back and fired on Corona so hard that his jaw shattered in pieces.

Macho

"Mujeres y muchachos! I have the package," Macho announced, as he reached down and grabbed the unconscious drug-lab manager.

"Good. We got everyone else, baby. Now hurry up and get out so I can set the time on the big bang," he heard Yessy tell him.

"Alrighty then, my love. I'm on the way out now. See you in a second," he told her.

Just then, Macho heard a whistle come from behind him. With the man slumped over his shoulder, Macho turned around and found himself looking at the end of a Mossberg pump shotgun, held by a hefty man, wearing a ski-mask fitted with a respirator over his mouth hole.

"Um…any chance you're here to help?" asked Macho, staring the man in his eyes.

The masked man shook his head no, then…

BOOM!

The Mossberg blew Macho backwards, putting him down on the floor. The close-range blast hit him so hard that everything in his midsection felt broken.

He couldn't move. He couldn't breathe. He laid there in agonizing pain.

He heard footsteps then. He looked up and saw the man again, hovering over him, with the 12-gauge in his hands.

"Antonio? What was that sound?" he heard his woman ask frantically through his earpiece.

Macho locked eyes with the man for a long awkward moment.

"Bae? Where are you? Talk to me!"

"You should've minded your own business, bitch ass nigga," the figure then said before raising the shotty up and pointing it at Macho's face. "And by the way, I hear you been lookin' for me. Well, here I am, nigga."

BOCCA! BOCKA! BOCKA! BOCKA! BOCKA! BOCKA!

To Be Continued…

Lock Down Publications and Ca$h Presents Assisted Publishing Packages

Due to an increase in the price of services we have increased our prices. The prices below reflect the price increase as of 11/1/24.

BASIC PACKAGE	UPGRADED PACKAGE
$699 Editing Cover Design Formatting	**$1000** Typing Editing Cover Design Formatting Upload eBooks to Amazon Upload Paperback to Amazon
ADVANCE PACKAGE **$1,400** Typing Editing (line editing/content) Cover Design Formatting Copyright Registration Proofreading Upload eBooks to Amazon Upload Paperback to Amazon	**LDP SUPREME PACKAGE** **$1,700** Typing Editing (line editing/content) Cover Design Formatting Copyright Registration Proofreading Set up Amazon Account Upload eBooks to Amazon Upload Paperback to Amazon Advertise on LDP's Amazon and Facebook Page

***

Other services available upon request. Additional charges may apply

Lock Down Publications
P.O. Box 944
Stockbridge, GA 30281-9998
Phone: 470 303-9761
Email: lockdownpublications@gmail.com

Submission Guideline

Submit the first three chapters of your completed manuscript to ldpsubmissions@gmail.com. In the subject line add **Your Book's Title**. The manuscript must be in a Word Doc file and sent as an attachment. Document should be in Times New Roman, double spaced, and in size 12 font. Also, provide your synopsis and full contact information. If sending multiple submissions, they must each be in a separate email.

Have a story but no way to send it electronically? You can still submit to LDP/Ca$h Presents. Send in the first three chapters, written or typed, of your completed manuscript to:

LDP: Submissions Dept
P.O. Box 944
Stockbridge, GA 30281-9998

DO NOT send original manuscript. Must be a duplicate. Provide your synopsis and a cover letter containing your full contact information.

Thanks for considering LDP and Ca$h Presents.

NEW RELEASES

BLOODLINE OF A SAVAGE 1-3
THESE VICIOUS STREETS 1-3
RELENTLESS GOON 1-3
SOULLESS GOON 1&2
BY PRINCE A. TAUHID

THE BUTTERFLY MAFIA 3
BY FUMIYA PAYNE

A THUG'S STREET PRINCESS 1&2
BY MEESHA

CITY OF SMOKE 1-3
BY MOLOTTI

GET IT IN SLUGS 1 &2
BY B. STALL

STANDING ON HER BUSINESS 1&2
BY DG SANTANA

STEPPERS 1,2&3
THE REAL BADDIES OF CHI-RAQ 1-3
BY KING RIO

THE LANE 1-3
BY KEN-KEN SPENCE

THUG OF SPADES 1&2
LOVE IN THE TRENCHES 1&2
CORNER BOYS 1&2
ONCE YOU GO GANGSTA
PROTÉGÉ OF A LEGEND 1- 3
BY COREY ROBINSON

TIL DEATH 3
BY ARYANNA

THE BIRTH OF A GANGSTER 4
BY DELMONT PLAYER

PRODUCT OF THE STREETS 1-3
BY DEMOND "MONEY" ANDERSON

MONEY HUNGRY DEMONS 1-2
BY TRANAY ADAMS

TRAP STARS
BY B. SHELLY

HUB CITY MENACE 1-4
BY J. WHITE

A THUGGISH PASSION 1&2
LAND OF DA HOOLIGANZ 1-4
KILLAZ ON STANDBY 1&2
FRESH OFF DA PORCH 1-3
SECURE DA BAG
AMBITIONS OF A SLIDER
FOR MY ENEMIES SAKE
SOULLESS GOON 1&2
FO'EVA ROLLIN 1-4
BY ASSA RAYMOND BAKER

THE LEVEL UP 1&2
BY LUXURY KING

HUNGRY FOR MONEY 1&2
SLIMBOS

QUEEN OF NAPTOWN 1&2
THA TAKEOVER 1-3
BY KEITH CHANDLER

DRILL CITY 1&2
BY ZAY'TOWVEN

LOVE ME OR LET ME GO
BY R. FACEY

SAVAGE DREAMZ
BY KING DAVID

MONEY AND DEAD HOMIES
BY DERRICK SUMMERS

A THUGS STREET PRINCESS 3 Coming Soon
BY MEESHA

BETRAYAL OF A G 2
BY RAY VINCI

SAVAGE FAMILY EMPIRE 1&2
SOULLESS GOON 1&2
THE DIRTY SIDE OF MONEY 1,2&3
BY PRINCE

BY THE TRUCKLOAD 1&2
TIPPIN' THE SCALES 1-4
BAD BITCHES WIT GUNZ 1-3
PROBLEM SOLVED 1-3
THE GIRLRILLA AND HER N*GGA
THE SINGLE LADIES
DYIN' TO GET RICH
THE GIRLRILLA AND HER N*GGA
BY CHRISTOPHER "DIESEL" HORNEZES

AVAILABLE NOW

RESTRAINING ORDER 1 & 2
BY CA$H & COFFEE

LOVE KNOWS NO BOUNDARIES 1-3
BY COFFEE

RAISED AS A GOON I, II, III & IV
BRED BY THE SLUMS I, II, III
BLAST FOR ME I & II
ROTTEN TO THE CORE I II III
A BRONX TALE I, II, III
DUFFLE BAG CARTEL I II III IV V VI
HEARTLESS GOON I II III IV V
A SAVAGE DOPEBOY I II
DRUG LORDS I II III
CUTTHROAT MAFIA I II
KING OF THE TRENCHES
BY GHOST

LAY IT DOWN I & II
LAST OF A DYING BREED I II
BLOOD STAINS OF A SHOTTA I & II III
BY JAMAICA

LOYAL TO THE GAME I II III
LIFE OF SIN I, II III
BY TJ & JELISSA

IF LOVING HIM IS WRONG…I & II
LOVE ME EVEN WHEN IT HURTS I II III
BY JELISSA

PUSH IT TO THE LIMIT
BY BRE' HAYES

GETTIN' MONEY BY THE TRUCKLOAD | DIESEL

BLOODY COMMAS I & II
SKI MASK CARTEL I, II & III
KING OF NEW YORK I II, III IV V
RISE TO POWER I II III
COKE KINGS I II III IV V
BORN HEARTLESS I II III IV
KING OF THE TRAP I II
BY T.J. EDWARDS

WHEN THE STREETS CLAP BACK I & II III
THE HEART OF A SAVAGE I II III IV
MONEY MAFIA I II
LOYAL TO THE SOIL I II III
BY JIBRIL WILLIAMS

A DISTINGUISHED THUG STOLE MY HEART I II & III
LOVE SHOULDN'T HURT I II III IV
RENEGADE BOYS 1-4
PAID IN KARMA 1-3
SAVAGE STORMS 1-3
AN UNFORESEEN LOVE 1-3
BABY, I'M WINTERTIME COLD 1-3
A THUG'S STREET PRINCESS 1,2&3
EMBRACING THE LOVE OF A BOSS 1&2
BY MEESHA

A GANGSTER'S CODE 1-3
A GANGSTER'S SYN 1-3
THE SAVAGE LIFE 1-3
CHAINED TO THE STREETS 1-3
BLOOD ON THE MONEY 1-3
A GANGSTA'S PAIN 1-3
BEAUTIFUL LIES AND UGLY TRUTHS
CHURCH IN THESE STREETS
BY J-BLUNT

CUM FOR ME 1-8
AN LDP EROTICA COLLABORATION

BLOOD OF A BOSS 1-5
SHADOWS OF THE GAME
TRAP BASTARD
BY ASKARI

THE STREETS BLEED MURDER 1-3
THE HEART OF A GANGSTA 1-3
BY JERRY JACKSON

WHEN A GOOD GIRL GOES BAD
BY ADRIENNE

THE COST OF LOYALTY 1-3
BY KWELI

BRIDE OF A HUSTLA 1-3
THE FETTI GIRLS 1-3
CORRUPTED BY A GANGSTA 1-4
BLINDED BY HIS LOVE
THE PRICE YOU PAY FOR LOVE 1-3
DOPE GIRL MAGIC 1-3
BY DESTINY SKAI

A KINGPIN'S AMBITION
A KINGPIN'S AMBITION II
I MURDER FOR THE DOUGH
BY AMBITIOUS

TRUE SAVAGE 1-7
DOPE BOY MAGIC 1-3
MIDNIGHT CARTEL 1-3
CITY OF KINGZ 1&2
NIGHTMARE ON SILENT AVE
THE PLUG OF LIL MEXICO 1&2
CLASSIC CITY
BY CHRIS GREEN

BACK IN BLOOD 1&2
SEX, MURDER AND GOD 1&2
COUNTDOWN OF A KILLA 1&2
GUNS DOWN, BOTTOMS UP 1&2
DEATH OF A SIDE CHICK
BY LO-LIFE

A GANGSTER'S REVENGE 1-4
THE BOSS MAN'S DAUGHTERS 1-5
A SAVAGE LOVE 1&2
BAE BELONGS TO ME 1&2
A HUSTLER'S DECEIT 1-3
WHAT BAD BITCHES DO 1-3
SOUL OF A MONSTER 1-3
KILL ZONE
A DOPE BOY'S QUEEN 1-3
TIL DEATH 1-3
IMMA DIE BOUT MINE 1-6
DYING FOR LIKES 1&2
KILLA CREW 1&2
BY ARYANNA

WHITE BOYS 1&2
BY BANDEMIC

A DOPEBOY'S PRAYER
BY EDDIE "WOLF" LEE

THE KING CARTEL 1-3
BY FRANK GRESHAM

THESE NIGGAS AIN'T LOYAL 1-3
BY NIKKI TEE

GANGSTA SHYT 1-3
BY CATO

THE ULTIMATE BETRAYAL
BY PHOENIX

BOSS'N UP 1-3
BY ROYAL NICOLE

I LOVE YOU TO DEATH
BY DESTINY J

I RIDE FOR MY HITTA
I STILL RIDE FOR MY HITTA
BY MISTY HOLT

LOVE & CHASIN' PAPER
BY QAY CROCKETT

TO DIE IN VAIN
SINS OF A HUSTLA
BY ASAD

BROOKLYN HUSTLAZ
BY BOOGSY MORINA

BROOKLYN ON LOCK 1 & 2
BY SONOVIA

GANGSTA CITY
BY TEDDY DUKE

A DRUG KING AND HIS DIAMOND 1-3
A DOPEMAN'S RICHES
HER MAN, MINE'S TOO 1&2
CASH MONEY HO'S
THE WIFEY I USED TO BE 1&2
PRETTY GIRLS DO NASTY THINGS
BY NICOLE GOOSBY

LIPSTICK KILLAH 1-3
CRIME OF PASSION 1-3
FRIEND OR FOE 1-3
BY MIMI

TRAPHOUSE KING 1-3
KINGPIN KILLAZ 1-3
STREET KINGS 1&2
PAID IN BLOOD 1&2
CARTEL KILLAZ 1-3
DOPE GODS 1&2
BY HOOD RICH

THE STREETS ARE CALLING
BY DUQUIE WILSON

STEADY MOBBN' 1-3
THE STREETS STAINED MY SOUL 1-3
BY MARCELLUS ALLEN

WHO SHOT YA 1-3
SON OF A DOPE FIEND 1-4
HEAVEN GOT A GHETTO 1&2
SKI MASK MONEY 1&2
BY RENTA

GORILLAZ IN THE BAY 1-4
TEARS OF A GANGSTA 1/&2
3X KRAZY 1&2
STRAIGHT BEAST MODE 1&2
BY DE'KARI

TRIGGADALE 1-3
MURDA WAS THE CASE 1-3
BY ELIJAH R. FREEMAN

SLAUGHTER GANG 1-3
RUTHLESS HEART 1-3
BY WILLIE SLAUGHTER

MARRIED TO A BOSS 1-3
BY DESTINY SKAI & CHRIS GREEN

GOD BLESS THE TRAPPERS 1-3
THESE SCANDALOUS STREETS 1-3
FEAR MY GANGSTA 1-5
THESE STREETS DON'T LOVE NOBODY 1-2
BURY ME A G 1-5
A GANGSTA'S EMPIRE 1-4
THE DOPEMAN'S BODYGAURD 1&2
THE REALEST KILLAZ 1-3
THE LAST OF THE OGS 1-3
BY TRANAY ADAMS

KINGZ OF THE GAME 1-7
CRIME BOSS 1-4
BY PLAYA RAY

FUK SHYT
BY BLAKK DIAMOND

DON'T F#CK WITH MY HEART 1&2
BY LINNEA

ADDICTED TO THE DRAMA 1-3
IN THE ARM OF HIS BOSS
BY JAMILA

LOYALTY AIN'T PROMISED 1&2
BY KEITH WILLIAMS

YAYO 1-4
A SHOOTER'S AMBITION 1&2
BRED IN THE GAME
BY S. ALLEN

TRAP GOD 1-3
RICH $AVAGE 1-3
MONEY IN THE GRAVE 1-3
CARTEL MONEY 1&2
BY MARTELL TROUBLESOME BOLDEN

FOREVER GANGSTA 1&2
GLOCKS ON SATIN SHEETS 1&2
BY ADRIAN DULAN

TOE TAGZ 1-4
LEVELS TO THIS SHYT 1&2
IT'S JUST ME AND YOU
BY AH'MILLION

KINGPIN DREAMS 1-3
RAN OFF ON DA PLUG
BY PAPER BOI RARI

THE STREETS MADE ME 1-3
BY LARRY D. WRIGHT

CONFESSIONS OF A GANGSTA 1-4
CONFESSIONS OF A JACKBOY 1-3
CONFESSIONS OF A HITMAN
CONFESSIONS OF A DOPE BOY
BY NICHOLAS LOCK

I'M NOTHING WITHOUT HIS LOVE
SINS OF A THUG
TO THE THUG I LOVED BEFORE
A GANGSTA SAVED XMAS
IN A HUSTLER I TRUST
BY MONET DRAGUN

QUIET MONEY 1-3
THUG LIFE 1-3
EXTENDED CLIP 1&2
A GANGSTA'S PARADISE
BY TRAI'QUAN

CAUGHT UP IN THE LIFE 1-3
THE STREETS NEVER LET GO 1-3
BY ROBERT BAPTISTE

NEW TO THE GAME 1-3
MONEY, MURDER & MEMORIES 1-3
BY MALIK D. RICE

CREAM 2-3
THE STREETS WILL TALK
BY YOLANDA MOORE

THE STREETS WILL NEVER CLOSE 1-3
BY K'AJJI

LIFE OF A SAVAGE 1-4
A GANGSTA'S QUR'AN 1-4
MURDA SEASON 1-3
GANGLAND CARTEL 1-3
CHI'RAQ GANGSTAS 1-4
KILLERS ON ELM STREET 1-3
JACK BOYZ N DA BRONX 1-3
A DOPEBOY'S DREAM 1-3
JACK BOYS VS DOPE BOYS 1-3
COKE GIRLZ
COKE BOYS
SOSA GANG 1&2
BRONX SAVAGES
BODYMORE KINGPINS
BLOOD OF A GOON
BY ROMELL TUKES

CONCRETE KILLA 1-3
VICIOUS LOYALTY 1-3
BLOODY MONEY BAGS 1&2
BY KINGPEN

NIGHTMARES OF A HUSTLA 1-3
BLOOD AND GAMES 1&2
BY KING DREAM

THE ULTIMATE SACRIFICE 1-6
KHADIFI
IF YOU CROSS ME ONCE 1-3
ANGEL 1-4
IN THE BLINK OF AN EYE
BY ANTHONY FIELDS

THE LIFE OF A HOOD STAR
BY CA$H & RASHIA WILSON

HARD AND RUTHLESS 1&2
MOB TOWN 251
THE BILLIONAIRE BENTLEYS 1-3
REAL G'S MOVE IN SILENCE
BY VON DIESEL

MOB TIES 1-7
SOUL OF A HUSTLER, HEART OF A KILLER 1-3
GORILLAZ IN THE TRENCHES
OPPS CRY TOO 1-3
THE DAUGHTER OF A CARTEL BOSS 1&2
BY SAYNOMORE

BODYMORE MURDERLAND 1-3
THE BIRTH OF A GANGSTER 1-4
TOP OF THE TRENCHES
BY DELMONT PLAYER

FOR THE LOVE OF A BOSS 1&2
BY C. D. BLUE

LOVE ME OR LET ME GO 1&2
BY R. FACEY

KILLA KOUNTY 1-5
TENDER 1&2
TREACHEROUS YN
BY KHUFU

MOBBED UP 1-4
THE BRICK MAN 1-5
THE COCAINE PRINCESS 1-10
STEPPERS 1-3
SUPER GREMLIN 1-5
A GANGSTA'S SON
THE CONNECT'S SECRET
BY KING RIO

MONEY GAME 1&2
BY SMOOVE DOLLA

A GANGSTA'S KARMA 1-5
BY FLAME
BLOOD AND MAYHEM
BY JJ DORSEY
KING OF THE TRENCHES 1-3
By GHOST & TRANAY ADAMS

QUEEN OF THE ZOO 1&2
BY BLACK MIGO

GRIMEY WAYS 1-3
BETRAYAL OF A G
BY RAY VINCI

XMAS WITH AN ATL SHOOTER
BY CA$H & DESTINY SKAI

KING KILLA 1&2
PAPER, ROCK, SNAKES
BY VINCENT "VITTO" HOLLOWAY

BETRAYAL OF A THUG 1&2
BY FRE$H

COUNTDOWN OF A KILLA 1&2
SEX, MURDER AND GOD 1&2
GUNS DOWN, BOTTOMS UP 1&2
BY LO-LIFE

FOR THE LOVE OF BLOOD 1-4
BY JAMEL MITCHELL

HOOD CONSIGLIERE 1-3
NO TIME FOR ERROR 1&2
REAL
BY KEESE

THE PLUG'S RUTHLESS DAUGHTER 1,2&3
REDEMPTION IN THE STREETS
BY TONY DANIELS

BORN IN THE GRAVE 1-3
CRIME PAYS 1-3
By Self Made Tay

MOAN IN MY MOUTH
BY XTASY

TORN BETWEEN A GANGSTER AND A GENTLEMAN
BY J-BLUNT

LOYALTY IS EVERYTHING 1-3
CITY OF SMOKE 1-3
BY MOLOTTI

HERE TODAY GONE TOMORROW 1&2
BY FLY ROCK

THE BUTTERFLY MAFIA 1-3
SALUTE MY SAVAGERY 1&2
BY FUMIYA PAYNE

WOMEN LIE MEN LIE 1-4
FIFTY SHADES OF SNOW 1-3
STACK BEFORE YOU SPLURGE
GIRLS FALL LIKE DOMINOES
NAÏVE TO THE STREETS
BY ROY MILLIGAN

PILLOW PRINCESS
BY S. HAWKINS

THE LANE 1&2
BY KEN-KEN SPENCE

THE PUSSY TRAP 1-5
BY NENE CAPRI

DIRTY DNA
BY BLAQUE

SANCTIFIED AND HORNY
BY XTASY

THE RUTHLESS LIFE
HIDEOUS
BY TOMMY COOK

BOOKS BY LDP'S CEO, CA$H

TRUST IN NO MAN
TRUST IN NO MAN 2
TRUST IN NO MAN 3
BONDED BY BLOOD
SHORTY GOT A THUG
THUGS CRY
THUGS CRY 2
THUGS CRY 3
TRUST NO BITCH
TRUST NO BITCH 2
TRUST NO BITCH 3
TIL MY CASKET DROPS
RESTRAINING ORDER
RESTRAINING ORDER 2
IN LOVE WITH A CONVICT
LIFE OF A HOOD STAR
XMAS WITH AN ATL SHOOTER

www.ingramcontent.com/pod-product-compliance
Lightning Source LLC
La Vergne TN
LVHW020714110826
845149LV00012B/2261

* 9 7 8 1 9 7 1 7 7 0 2 2 2 *